GHOSTS AND GADGETS

The Raven Mysteries

Also by Marcus Sedgwick
for older readers

Blood Red, Snow White
The Book of Dead Days
The Dark Flight Down
The Dark Horse
The Dead Days Omnibus
Floodland
The Foreshadowing
The Kiss of Death
Revolver
My Swordhand is Singing
Witch Hill

The Raven Mysteries

Flood and Fang

Visit Marcus Sedgwick's website at –
www.marcussedgwick.com

and for more on the Raven Mysteries, go to -
www.ravenmysteries.co.uk

GHOSTS AND GADGETS

The Raven Mysteries

Book 2

MARCUS SEDGWICK

Illustrated by Pete Williamson

Orion
Children's Books

First published in Great Britain in 2009
by Orion Children's Books
a division of the Orion Publishing Group Ltd
Orion House
5 Upper St Martin's Lane
London WC2H 9EA
A Hachette UK Company

1 3 5 7 9 10 8 6 4 2

A catalogue record for this book is available from the British Library.

ISBN 978 1 84255 694 8

Printed in Great Britain by
CPI Mackays, Chatham ME5 8TD

www.orionbooks.co.uk

For Joseph and William

One

Castle Otherhand
is home to
all sorts of
oddballs, lunatics
and fruitcakes.
It's just as well
for all of them
that they have
a secret weapon:
he's called Edgar.

Is my beak wonky?

This is a question  which vexes me more and more these days, though I think it was almost ten years ago when I first caught myself going cross-eyed at two thousand feet trying to look down the length of my foremost extremity.

Now, vain bird that I am, I find myself squinting into the ornate looking glass above the mantel in the dining room a little too often, trying to establish for once and all whether my beak is curved. It never used to be, not when I was a fledgling. You could have drawn technical diagrams with the thing! It was like a ruler! But now, ah now, I'm not so sure.

It was on just such a pondering that I embarked one fateful night that was to become the start of a most dreadful and frightsome episode in Otherhand history. An adventure so quiverful that I scare myself now to speak of it, and yet, as guardian and custodian of all things Otherhand, relate it I must!

I pecked the mirror one last time, just to give the old bird in the glass a warning:

Keep your marbles, Edgar, and forget

about your beak for five minutes.

'Is the crow losing it?'

I turned to see Minty pointing a fork at me. Something dropped from the fork on to the carpet and Fellah was on it like a flash.

'Cudweed! Control your monkey,' Solstice said, sighing.

'Anything that hits the floor is his,' Cudweed protested. 'We agreed!'

'*You* agreed,' Solstice said, tutting.

It was Sunday evening, and the whole odd lot of them were gathered at dinner.

Lord Valevine was at the head of the enormous dining table. About a delicate stone's throw away sat Minty, at the other end. Between them, on a table that could have seated forty with plenty of elbow room, were the other five members of the Otherhand family: Solstice and Cudweed, on opposite sides of the table, Fizz and Buzz, clamped into high chairs and not crawling over every conceivable surface, and Grandma Slivinkov, somewhere in the middle, sitting bolt upright, partly because that was how she'd been brought up, but mostly because she was tied to the back of her chair so she didn't fall asleep in her soup. Something had to be done about it after the fourth time.

Now while this seating arrangement was not entirely convenient, it did at least mean that the various egos of the family were separated by some good safe distances. And there are always plenty of maids to run around with plates and dishes and whatnot.

On some evenings,
the distance between the diners
gave us lots of fun, and sometimes
there'd be much laughter as Lord Otherhand
would have me fly the salt cellar down to Lady
Otherhand; the weighty condiment clutched in
my claws, and then return with a celery fork
held in my powerful beak.

Everyone would applaud these little feats
of my skill, and now and then for good measure,
I'd throw in an extra trick or two,
like pretending to drop the finest
crystal glass, only to catch it again
before injury occurred to either bird or beaker.

It has to be said that those days are
less frequent.

For one thing, there's the monkey. Since he arrived, my parlour games have been curtailed. That mentally-challenged baboon goes 'ape', if I may mix my primates so wilfully, if I get so much as a whisper of appreciation, and the thought of the fights we've had around the silverware makes me shudder.

For another thing . . .

Well, it can only be said that strange things are afoot in Castle Otherhand. That evening, the family were a discontented, tetchy and downright irritable crew. Each and every one seemed wrapped up in their own thoughts: Minty with her latest fad, which involved needles and thread, Cudweed with his awful orang-utan, Lord Valevine with gloomy thoughts that had something to do with money and the lack of it, Solstice with . . . well, I don't know what.

Outside, the sky had grown black, and I could sense, from a tingle in my beak, that a storm was brewing. A big storm.

Minty stabbed mercilessly at something else on her plate, and began waving her fork at me again. Fellah sat drooling on the carpet, and Solstice glowered at Cudweed, who stuck his tongue out at his sister. Nonetheless, he slipped a lead round Fellah's foot, before he could make a lunge for anyone's dinner.

'I said, is the crow losing it?'

'What's that?' Valevine spluttered, lifting his gaze from the tablecloth. 'The crow?'

Suddenly everyone was staring at me.

Fighting a desperate urge to hunt for fleas, I flapped across the room and landed on the handle of a vast and silvery ornamental punch bowl, where I tried to strike a pose that said: **I am aloof**.

'What's the difference between a crow and a raven?' Cudweed asked no one in particular.

'Oh, not one of your jokes, puh-lease,' groaned Solstice. She flumped forward rather sulkily, her elbows on the table.

Grandma Slivinkov opened an eye.

'I like jokes,' she said, and opened her other eye in readiness.

Everyone looked at her, if only because it was the first time she'd spoken in three weeks.

But if they expected more, they were disappointed. Eyes turned back on Cudweed.

'No, I just mean, what's the difference between a crow and a raven?'

'If you have to tell jokes, please get it over with quickly,' Solstice said, flicking a pea which hit Fellah. Deliberately, I hoped.

'Hey!' cried Cudweed. 'Don't abuse my monkey!'

'Don't shout at the dinner table.' Minty waved a finger at Cudweed.

Valevine coughed, and leaned forward, then in a loud voice, declared:

'All ravens are crows, but not all crows are ravens.'

There was more than a moment's silence, then Grandma S began to chuckle.

'Heh heh heh,' she went. I promise you, it was just like that, 'heh heh heh'.

Cudweed and Solstice exchanged glances.

'I don't get it,' Solstice said.

'That's probably because it's rude, dear,' said Minty, glaring at her husband.

'It's because it's not a joke!' said Cudweed.

'You can say that again,' said Solstice.

'Heh heh heh. Heh heh heh,' went old lady Slivinkov.

'Noo-oo-oo,' moaned Cudweed, making at least three syllables out of the word, but before

he could open his mouth again he was shushed
by Minty.

Valevine addressed the table again.

'All ravens are crows, but not all crows
are ravens. Isn't that right, Edgar?'

And I was just about to open my beak and
give a loud '**caw**' of agreement, when the storm
broke over the castle.

A flash of lightning right outside the
window lit the dim dining room like a summer's
day, and then was gone, but before we'd even

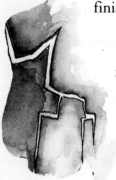

finished blinking, the thunder arrived.

Not one of those low stomach
rumblings that you sometimes
hear from the other side of the
mountain, but a painfully loud

clap, right above
our heads.

'Futhork!' I said, swearing badly
in the old raven tongue. Fortunately none of the
family knows what it means, or I might have been
sent to my cage without supper.

Pandemonium broke out with that thunder
and lightning, followed by the most gargantuan
storm I've witnessed in many a long year. In an
instant, the whole room was in chaos and . . .

. . . And, well, actually.

This is, er, difficult to admit. It pains me
rather, and I might be exaggerating somewhat,
because actually most of the room was calm.
Valevine, Minty, the children, even the terrible
toddlers were all quite happy in the face of the

electrical storm. Grandma Slivinkov had actually gone to sleep again, though I think she might have muttered 'Heh heh heh' once or twice.

So when I say the whole room was reduced to panic and mayhem, I am in fact referring to only two creatures: myself, and that damn monkey.

I wouldn't want you to get the wrong idea, because it's been well-proven that I am a fearless and proud raven, but I seem to have developed a dread and mortal fear of thunder and lightning. Even the merest hint of it and I become demented.

I jumped onto the table cloth and began to peck my reflection in the punch bowl repeatedly, and with a demonic desperation.

'He *has* gone loopy,' Minty
said, but that was the last thing I
heard anyone say clearly. Fellah,
and this is the part that really shames
me, that we might be in any way similar, had by
now also scrambled his eggs, and was leaping and
shrieking as if his tail was on fire.

In a moment he'd pulled out of Cudweed's
slippery grip, and was off around the dining room
on a tour of destruction, gibbering and swiping
at anything and everyone.

Meanwhile, I think I'd
given up on the punch bowl and
was banging the side of my head
against the tabletop. Please don't ask me
why. I think it might have been to occupy

the fear sensors in my brain with something other than the storm. Either that or I had indeed gone screwy, as Minty suggested.

In another second, Fellah had bolted for the door.

Flinch, that most unresponsive of butlers, made a half-hearted effort to stoop, but the ape was through his legs like a rat on roller skates, and away.

Cudweed was after him in a flash, quite impressive for a boy of his dimensions, and then all hell *did* break out.

'Cudweed!' screamed Minty at the top of her voice. 'You must ask to be excused! Uh! Get me that boy!'

She stormed off, rounding up a search party of maids, headed by Cook, to bring the boy to heel.

Outside, the storm raged and rioted. I decided to hit my head on the table a little harder to see if that would help.

It didn't.

The last thing I heard was Solstice appealing to her father.

'Father,' she said, 'what *is* the difference between a crow and a raven?'

Two

What is Valevine's most useless invention? The automatic rowing machine, too heavy to take anyone with it? The parasol made of ice, intended to keep you very cool? Or perhaps the Do-Not-Hit-Your-Head-On-This-Sign sign above the laboratory door?

All ravens are crows, but not all crows are ravens. I think that says something rather profound, yes?

Lord Valevine had pretty much nailed it with that one, but thinking back, perhaps I was the only other being in the room to understand what he'd said. Given that I realise a small percentage of you following this tale may not have feathers, let me explain what he meant.

I will try to think of a human equivalent.

Ah ha!

All kings are men, but not all men are kings. See? Not so hard after all.

Solstice, being the diligent girl that she is, had decided to tackle the problem herself. She lay on the wolfskin rug in her room, nose deep in a large and important-looking book.

I gazed about her room from her little
black velvet hung four-poster bed to the
newly-wallpapered east wall with its cheery
graveyard scene.

Outside the storm still growled and
flashed, flashed and growled, and the rain

hammered against the octagonal window that overlooks the valley. The fire crackled in the grate, and Solstice had a big mug of hot milk and honey steaming at her elbow. It was her favourite mug too, a heavy dark brown thing with a skull grinning on the side of it.

I gathered that I had squawked so badly in the dining room that the rest of dinner had been cancelled, and I'd been sent to my cage in the Red Room. Apparently, I'd made such a fuss at the thought of being shut up by myself that they'd relented. I hadn't become my normal smooth self again until they said I could spend the night in Solstice's room, which meant Flinch had had to carry my cage from the Red Room to Solstice's.

I was jittery still, and rubbed my beak on the bars occasionally if I thought Solstice had forgotten about me.

But she hadn't. Bless her, the dear girl was finding out about ravens. Long overdue, too.

She read from the book.

Less of the 'common', if you don't mind, I thought, still surprised that Solstice was reading about ravens and not reciting morbid poetry as she usually does.

"'. . . is also known as the Northern Raven . . .'"

That's more like it, I cawed.

"'. . . and is a large all-black bird belonging to the crow family, known as the . . .'"

She stumbled over the word, but it is, in fairness, a tricky one.

"'. . . the Corvidae.' Hum, Edgar. That sounds posh. Are you a posh bird?'

I gave a slight shrug which meant, yes, I suppose I might be if you care to mention it.

She read on.

"'As well as ravens, members of the Corvidae family include rooks, crows, magpies, jackdaws and choughs.'"

'Kawk,' I said quietly. I'm quite fond

of choughs, but magpies you can keep. Showy-offy birds. To emphasise my point, I said so.

'**Ark!**'

'"The Northern Raven's proper name is Corvus Corax." Oh, Edgar! You are posh! "They are medium to large birds . . ."'

Well, what can I say. I *have* been trying to cut back on seconds . . .

'". . . with strong feet and bills, and rictal bristles." I don't know what that means, do you, Edgar?'

I kept quiet because I've never heard of them either, but I suppose it means the little spiky feathers I have around my gape. Great for catching a grasshopper on the wing.

"'. . . In terms of feeding habits, Corvids are highly opportunistic foragers.'"

Well, I have to be, the pitiful way they feed me round here. Can I help it if I find myself in the kitchen staring at the hog roast from time to time?

"'Based on their brain to body ratio, Corvids are among . . .'"

Among? Pah!

"'. . . are among the most intelligent of all birds, with a quotient approaching that of the apes . . .'"

Oh, please no. Don't say I'm stupider than a monkey. If Cudweed finds that out . . .

"'. . . and only beaten by humans.'"

They can't have met Cudweed, eh, Edgar?' said Solstice, winking at me. She chuckled to herself.

'Hey, Edgar, listen to this bit. "Corvidae are also among the few species on the planet to make use of tools. Outside of the human species, tool use has only been noted in primates (that's monkeys, I think) and the crow family. It has recently been proved that the tool use of crows is more sophisticated even than that of chimpanzees."

Ha! Wait till we tell Cudweed that bit! "Such tool use includes choosing and shaping sticks to assist in scavenging and foraging behaviour."'

Solstice stopped reading, and looked up at me.

'Why, Edgar,' she said, 'I had no idea you were so clever. Is it true? Can you really select and shape a stick?'

She came over to the cage and tickled my tail feathers.

Yes, I nodded, I can use a stick. And I can speak Latin and Greek, do really tricky fractions, and pick locks with my beak.

But I kept quiet about that lot.

Solstice smiled at me really quite nicely, displaying her rather lovely white teeth, and a second later, all the warriors of Valhalla burst through the door. At least, Cudweed and Fellah did, and they made an extraordinary sight, for their hair, both monkey's and boy's, was sticking straight up in the air.

Cudweed opened his mouth.

'A guh,' he said.

Then he tried again. He pointed nowhere in particular.

'A guh-guh-guh.'

Then he fainted on the carpet.

Three

Some families say
they have skeletons
in the cupboard. The
Otherhands actually
do, which gave the
vicar a nasty shock
when he came to stay
one weekend.

It took Cudweed more than twelve hours to come round from his fainting fit, though as he was carried by Flinch and put to bed, it's my suspicion that the lazy boy just went straight from his coma into a good night's sleep, thank you very much. A good night's sleep that no one else benefited from, as we all spent the night pacing his bedroom and wondering first, what was wrong with him and second, when his hair would return to normal.

I say we all paced, but because ravens are not good at pacing, I decided the best thing I could do was sit on his head with my eyes shut and stay very still.

I may possibly have had forty winks, but I swear not one wink more.

The monkey presented an interesting case. I had never seen him so quiet and subdued. He even seemed to be completely uninterested in assaulting me, which is a rare thing indeed. Upon being returned to Cudweed's room, he lunged for the wardrobe, snuck inside and spent the night quivering among Cudweed's jumpers.

It was a long and weary-making night.

Valevine was
doing most of
the pacing and
a fair deal of muttering too.
Between snoozes, I eavesdropped on his woes,
and it made for chilling listening. It's a well
known fact that the Otherhands are not as
wealthy as they once were. There are many
reasons for this, but the main one is that none of
them does anything that earns them any money.
For the last hundred years it appears we've been
living off a sum in a bank account in
Lichtenstein.

Recently, Valevine has had more and
more letters, letters in smart white envelopes
with foreign postmarks. With every one that he

opens his face falls more forlorn, then he props
the envelope behind the bust of Lord Deffreeque
in the Small Hall gallery, and rapidly forgets
about it.

But ignore the letters as he might, it seems
our money is running out, and though we have
a rather fine, if somewhat dilapidated, castle in
which to live, we have about eleventy-eight
servants to feed and
pay, and that's
before the mouths
and beaks of the
family itself get a
look in.

I admit
Spatchcock does a

little growing of vegetables in the walled garden, but not enough to feed all the slavering mouths in the castle.

Minty's concerns seemed by comparison more mundane, as she sat on the end of her son's bed, with a needle and some scraps of black velvet in her hands. She cut at the velvet with a hacky-hack pair of scissors, would stitch for a short time, and then throw the whole thing up in the air with a curse and a sigh. After three hours all she'd made was a fluffy black mess on the floor.

Two maids, Madeleine and Fifi, stood

nervously by the door, unsure whether they were required or not.

And Solstice? Well, she paced a bit with her father, and sat a bit with her mother, chewing her knuckles, and staring at Cudweed's hair from time to time.

'Edgar,' she whispered. 'What do you think is wrong with Cudweed?'

Well, I thought, do you want a list?

But I could see she was worried, and as she's as thin and sharp as a pin already I don't want her worrying more, so instead I said the most reassuring thing I could.

'**Urr.**'

That appeared to help her, and she tickled me under my beak, and then I decided to rest my eyes again for a brief spell.

Well, I must have slept for longer than I thought, because when I woke again, it was late morning.

Outside, the storm was over, and all was still and calm. A gentle beam or two of sunshine brushed Cudweed's brow, and he began to stir.

I shuffled on my hairy perch and gave a little '**ark**' to get everyone's attention.

'Oh! Valevine! Dearest! Cudweed is waking up!'

Minty clutched the poor boy's chubby

wrist and waited.

'Eh? What?' said Valevine, and turned from brooding at the window in time to see Solstice join her mother at the bedside.

'Cudweed? Oh, my boy, can you hear me? Are you quite delirious?'

Cudweed opened an eye, and sat up.

'What's for breakfast?' he said. 'Any chance of sausages?'

He blinked a couple of times, and then I swear you could hear his brain working. Noting all the people in his room: Valevine, Minty, Solstice, Flinch, Madeleine, Fifi, and yours truly, something began to worry him.

'Is it my birthday?' he asked tentatively, trying to work out why else we'd all be there.

'In that case, I really would like some sausages.'

No one said a word, but just stared at him all the harder.

There was another click and whirr from the boy's skull, and then he emitted a loud and piercing shriek, and disappeared under his sheets.

'What an extraordinary performance!' exclaimed Valevine, expressing a passing interest in his son. He peered at the bed, where a white mound shivered slightly.

'No, no!' cried Solstice. 'Don't you see? He's remembered about last night, about whatever it was that happened to him.'

As if in answer, the shivering mound gave an extra big wobble, and there was the hint of a moan.

Fellah the monkey seemed to be aware

that his lord and master was awake again, and

chose this moment to leave the wardrobe.

He shot across the room like

a greased pig, and bolted

under the covers to join

Cudweed.

Well, that was enough for Cudweed.

Surprised beyond all measure, he gave another

loud scream and jumped out of bed, landing an

impressive distance away.

'A guh!' he cried. 'A guh. A guh. A guh!'

'A what?' asked Solstice, but this only

upset Cudweed further.

'A guh!' he declared. 'A guh-guh-guh.'

He took a deep, deep breath, and tried

for one last time.

'A guh-guh-ghost!'

'What?'

'Yes! A ghost. A ghost! A ghost!'

Fellah chattered from the bed, and began to leap about in such a mental fashion that everyone stared at him now instead. The monkey hung his head grotesquely, and for an ugly monkey, he made an even more hideous face, all sagging jaw and goggly eyes. He waved his knuckles about by his feet, and then made a horrible, and frankly unnecessarily, chilling noise.

'Oooooo-ooo.'

'Oh, for heaven's sake!' exclaimed Valevine, heading for the door.

'No!' said Cudweed, pointing at his monkey. 'That's just what it was like. Just like that. Exactly. Almost.'

'Oooooo-ooo. Ooooo,' said Fellah, pleased with how much attention he was getting, I suspect.

'Oh, my dear goodness,' said Valevine. 'I cannot believe I have distracted myself from my studies for many valuable hours for this nonsense. I have work to do!'

'No!' cried Cudweed. 'Father! We really did see a guh . . . a horrible big, scary . . . guh. I swear we did. I went after Fellah, when he ran away because of the storm. He was really scared, and he ran really fast, but he'd put his feet in the soup so I followed his footprints for ages. He'd run for miles and miles, and I followed him into a bit of the castle where I've never been before. And I only caught up with him because he stopped at a corner. He was scared stiff! I ran up to him and looked round the corner and saw what he was looking at, and it was . . .'

'It was . . . ?' prompted Minty.

'It was . . .' stuttered Cudweed.

'The ghost?' asked Solstice.

Cudweed nodded furiously, and Madeleine and Fifi began to make small whimpering noises, whispering to each other about the ghostly business.

Valevine sighed so powerfully it

put the candles out, a thing someone else should have already seen to, since it was now bright and sunny outside.

'Oh, my dear boy. What an absurd amount of nonsense!'

'No!' cried Cudweed. 'No! It was a . . . and it was . . . and then we ran, and ran, and then we got to Solstice's room, and then I don't remember any more.'

'And tell me, dear boy,' said Valevine, looking at his watch, 'which precise part of the castle were you in?'

'Well, I've never been there before, but I suppose, I mean, I think, that I suppose that we were somewhere, more or less, in the, erm, South Wing . . .'

He trailed off.

'And do we, or do we not know,' Valevine said, using up the last of his small supply of patience, 'that the Lost South Wing of the castle is a law unto itself? That the wind can make strange noises in the empty corridors? That light can play off unpolished mirrors in a most peculiar fashion?'

Cudweed said nothing. Fellah was still doing his ghost impression, until I pecked him on the head from behind and made a speedy retreat to the safety of Solstice's arm. The maids still whispered, and I think I could hear Fifi's knees knocking rapidly together.

'Well?' asked Valevine, peering down at his small, trembling son.

'Yes, Father,' Cudweed said in a meek voice. 'But . . .'

'No buts!' Valevine said. 'Buts are for goats! Now, I have wasted enough of my time on this idiotic affair, and if we are all thrown into the street then it will really be no surprise whatsoever! Good day to you all!'

Valevine spun out of the room, slamming the door behind him.

A second later the door opened again,  and Lord Otherhand stuck his head back into the room.

'Some of those sausages seem like a good plan though.'

He left.

Cudweed turned to Minty, but she was already collecting her scraps of material from the floor.

'You believe me, don't you, Mother?'

'Mmm? Oh, yes, dear. Of course I do,' said Minty, in just that way mothers do when they haven't even heard you. She left without a backward glance, taking Flinch and the maids with her.

Cudweed turned to Solstice.

'Solstice, you believe me. Don't you?'

'Yes,' Solstice said, and Cudweed seemed a little happier, but I could tell that she didn't mean it.

And quite honestly, neither did I.

Yet.

Four

Box and Sons has
been the family's
faithful undertakers
for as long as anyone
can remember.
They're well known
for their calm
manner in the
face of even the
grisliest corpse.

The next few days were uneventful. Almost quiet.

No one believed what Cudweed claimed to have seen, and after a few days, exactly what he'd seen seemed to vary from account to account. And yet there was still an eerie air pervading the castle. Whisperings and gossipings, particularly in the kitchens, as maids discussed past sightings of spooks in Castle Otherhand, of grey ladies, headless horseman, white monks, and most frightful of all, the spectral sheep once seen jogging across the lawns.

I'm an old bird, I don't know if I've mentioned this before, but it's the case. I've seen a lot of oddness in Castle Otherhand, and before, when it

was Castle Deffreeque. Oddness is just part of the place, but ghosts? Well, that's another matter.

I mean to say, I've had my suspicions over the years, and if anywhere in the castle were to have supernatural denizens, then it would be the Lost South Wing, a rambling and ruinous assortment of crazy architecture that was thrown up over the course of a few hundred years, but which later fell into disuse and decay. Nowadays, no one goes there. Lord Valevine declared it unsafe after a series of highly scientific tests he made on the floorboards, and after everyone had helped pull Flinch back up through the holes in the floor, no one felt much like going in there anyway.

But that's not to say that we have ghosts at Otherhand. A castle with a personality of its own, yes. Ghosties, no.

Meanwhile, the sour mood in the castle seemed to have spread from the bottomless caves beneath the cellars, to the battlements and loftiest spires on the tallest towers.

One afternoon, Solstice and Cudweed sat on the High Terrace, having a snack at a picnic table overlooking the whole wonderful valley of Otherhand. The monkey sat by Cudweed's feet, and there was something about the fact he was still cowering almost a week after the event that unnerved me.

I alternated my time, perching near Solstice's

blood-orangeade, and circling above the others,

taking turns on some lovely updrafts. After a long day of sun on the thick granite, the castle itself can send wonderful warm currents of air up for me to glide upon, so strong that I perhaps have to flap only every minute or two.

From high above in his room at the top of the East Tower, the sounds of Valevine working on his latest invention drifted across and down to us. It's a curious thing that the East Tower is not actually in the east of the castle. One of the oddities of a castle that took centuries to build is that things move. Well, not that they move exactly, but once upon a time, the East Tower was in fact the eastern most point of the castle. But since other bits got added later, it's now pretty much in the middle. But names do not change, so the East Tower it is.

And from the East Tower came the familiar noise of Lord Otherhand at work.

Each thing he makes is more ludicrous than the last, and as usual there was a great hammering and drilling and swearing, but Solstice and Cudweed seemed unaware of it all. The children were in a subdued mood, and I made it my business to find out what was wrong.

'Solstice?' asked Cudweed. 'What did Father mean? That morning, when I woke up, after the You-Know-What?'

'About us being thrown on the streets?'

Cudweed nodded, and slurped his ginger beer.

'I think we might be in a bit of trouble,' Solstice said. 'It seems we're poorer than we thought. If we run out of money, we'll have to sell the castle. Go and live somewhere, well, normal.'

Cudweed shuddered.

'Normal?' he said, 'I don't think I'd like that.'

'Hum,' said Solstice.

I thought I'd better comfort the glum pair, so I landed on the end of the table, but made a bit of a hash of it. I tripped over a plate of muffins and landed beak first on the table. Unfortunately, the old bill got wedged in a crack, and for a moment I was stuck, until, laughing, Solstice pulled me free.

Cudweed joined her laughter, and I suppose I had cheered them up, but I stalked off to the end of the table and sulked for a bit, feeling old and stupid. While I tried to work out whether my accident had made the wonk in my beak better or worse, I listened over what passes for a shoulder in a raven.

'But what's Father going to do about it?' Cudweed said, after a long spell of tricky thinking.

Solstice sighed and pointed up at the East Tower.

'That,' she said, and Cudweed's face grew dark.

'Oh,' he said. 'What about Mother?'

Solstice almost screamed with frustration.

'Mother has become obsessed with sewing. All she does all day is snip and cut and sew and then throw the whole lot away and start again.

Flinch has been into town three times for more

black velvet already!'

'And meanwhile, we're to lose our home

and be scared to death into the bargain!'

It was possible. There was talk circulating

about an incident from a few years back when

the spectral sheep had struck unawares in the

rhubarb patch. Unpleasant.

Cudweed began to snivel. Most unattractive.

'There, Cudweed. Shh,' said Solstice. 'It

won't come to that. Otherhands have lived here

for centuries and I'm sure we always will.'

I didn't like to tell her that I'd heard

Lady Deffreeque say the very same thing to her

husband about two weeks before the Otherhands

invaded. But that was over three hundred years

ago, and long forgotten now, by all
except those of black feather and
wonky beak.

Still, she was trying to be a comfort to her
little brother.

'I'm sure we won't lose the castle,' she
said. 'And you know, Cudweed, there really
aren't any ghosts in the South Wing.'

That made Cudweed stop snivelling. He
sat up straight, and looked Solstice right in the eye.

'But there are. I saw one. So did Fellah.'

'But Cudweed . . .'

'But nothing! Look at him. Look at
Fellah! Have you ever seen him like this? Ever?'

Solstice looked at the monkey, and I
swivelled round for a proper inspection myself.

It was true. I suddenly realised that in a whole week that stinky chimp had not once tried to strangle, throttle, or otherwise murder me.

Something was definitely wrong, and the same thought seemed to have occurred to Solstice.

'Cudweed. Do you mean? Is it really true? Did you really see a ghost?'

Now it was Cudweed's turn to wail in frustration.

'Yes! Yes, yes, yes. Yes, I saw a You-Know-What! I thought you believed me!'

'Yes,' said Solstice rapidly. 'I did. But now I really, really do.'

She stood up.

'Gasp,' she declared, flicking her long black hair back over her shoulder. 'In that case, there's only one thing for it.'

'And what's that?' asked Cudweed, but if he didn't know what was coming, I had already guessed. Good luck to her, I thought. Have fun. Say hi to the ghosties. Tell us how you got on.

'Yes,' said Solstice. 'One thing. We must go into the South Wing and investigate!'

'We?' cried Cudweed. 'We? But I'm never going there again in my life!'

'No,' said Solstice, laughing. 'I know that! I don't mean "we", you and me, I mean "we", me and Edgar.

Isn't that right, Edgar?'

But I said nothing, because I was standing stock still on the battlements, trying to look like a gargoyle.

Sadly for me, it didn't work.

Five

It's said that
something lurks
in Otherhand Lake,
and though no one
agrees on exactly
what it might be,
it's not always a
good idea to go
boating at dusk.

I decided the best thing I could do in the circumstances was to sulk for a week or two, but it didn't work. Solstice was not to be distracted, dissuaded or otherwise dislodged from her self-appointed mission of investigating the ghosts.

I have to give her some credit though, because she appeared to be taking it seriously.

'If we're to be Ghost Hunters, Edgar,' she said to me one morning, 'we need to be properly organised for our expedition.'

And so Solstice prepared her Ghost Hunting Kit, which was as follows:

A small electric torch, with which to peer into the darkest crevices.

A pen and sketchbook, to note down

anything note-down-worthy.

A miniature tape recorder.

A little silver crucifix. Also a Star of
David, some glass rosary beads, an Egyptian
Ankh, a four-leaf clover and a somewhat moth-
eaten rabbit's foot. ('Well,' explained Solstice,
'who knows what Ghosties believe in?')

A scarf and gloves in case of exploration
anywhere chilly.

A peanut butter and cucumber sandwich.

A thermos of hot milk and honey.

A leather satchel to
carry everything in.

She laid
it all out on her
bedroom floor

and ticked each item off a list she'd made.

'Well, I wonder,' she announced. 'I wonder if that's everything you need for Ghost Hunting. I suppose it must be, because I can't think of anything else.'

She turned to me and smiled.

'Now come on, Edgar, it's time to stop sulking. You know I need you. I'd be too scared to go into the South Wing by myself, and you're the only one brave enough to come with me. Isn't that right?'

I'm a soft-hearted old bird and Solstice knows just how to wrap me round her little finger. But I still wasn't convinced.

'**Urk,**' I said, rather snappily.

'Edgar, please?' Solstice cooed. 'Okay

then, I'll make you a deal. I'll give you a dried
mouse if you come with me, yes?'

'**Ark**,' I stated.

'Okay then,' she said. 'Two dried mice.
But that's my final offer!'

I flopped off the bedpost and on to the
floor and tapped the satchel with my beak.

'Does that mean yes?' Solstice cried. 'Oh,
excellent! Very well, we'll just go past the stores
on the way and collect your mice, and then we
can be off. How exciting, Edgar! We are now
Ghost Hunters!'

Hmm, I thought, exciting is not the word
I would choose. But then I've lived in this castle
for an awfully long time, and I've seen more
oddness than I care to remember.

I tried to concentrate on the thought of dried mice, but all I could see with my inner eye was Fellah's impression of the hideous You-Know-What.

Six

An excerpt from Valevine's inventing notebook: Invent glue. Stick chairs back together. Find something else for elephants to sit on.

May I talk to you for a short while about the subject of smell?

Imagine a long line, with divisions along its length, known as a scale. The scale has two ends. At one end, we place nice smells. They are smells so nice that we don't even call them smells. We call them aromas, or perhaps even better yet, scents. The allure of evening primrose, of honeysuckle and other such charming flowers. We might also add along this end of the scale such beauties as angels' breath and summer breezes.

Somewhere along the line, according to personal preference, we could put in smells like strawberries, hot-dogs and breweries, petrol,

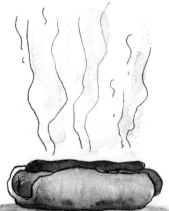

wet stone and
leather. These are all
extremely interesting
smells, especially when
you have as many nerve
endings up your conk as I
do, but while some people
like them, others do not.

And then I would ask you to consider
briefly bad smells. Unpleasant ones that are really
most disgusting. Drains, sewers and septic tanks,
for example. There too at this end of the scale
forty-two year old Stilton, elephant's breath and
rotting meat.

Hang on a minute, Edgar, you might say
to me, don't you eat rotting meat? Isn't that part

of your whole scavenging-carrion-thing?

And it's true, I would have to confess, but even I know that it stinks to high heaven, and before you ask how I can therefore eat such niffy food, let me briefly steer you in the direction of certain human food stuffs, like fermented herring, mussels, and Parmesan cheese.

Anyway, my point, and I do have one, is that if this is the foul and rank end of the odour scale, then somewhere a mile or two off this particular end of the scale is none other than Fellah, Cudweed's monkey.

So it was, as it often is, that as I came down the main staircase with Solstice, about to embark on our mission, I had very early warning of the presence of my arch enemy. Tendrils of stink shuffled their way up my bill and I gave a shudder of the feather.

Sure enough, as we reached the ground floor, there he was, still hanging around Cudweed's neck with his usual restricted IQ.

However, I concede that his behaviour did have some merit, because something quite interesting was going on in the Small Hall, namely that Lord Otherhand, ably assisted by Flinch, was emerging from the not-so-secret door that leads along and then up to the East Tower to Valevine's laboratory. Somewhere between them, they wrestled with a large and unlikely contraption that we all immediately took to be Valevine's latest invention.

It looked like a road accident between a

pram and science museum. It was mounted on wheels, and now that Valevine and Flinch had extracted it from the narrow stairwell, they trundled it proudly across the polar bear and tiger skin rugs that carpeted the Small Hall.

On top of the wheels sat an assortment of pipes, tubes, wires and dials. There were also,

 I should mention, switches, levers, knobs and buttons. Slung in a sort of undercarriage was a mighty array of batteries, to give the thing life, I supposed.

All in all it was
very impressive, although
at that point, we had no idea
what it was.

Lord Valevine
read our minds, some
faster than others, and
spun around with
a flourish.

'Ah! My fair children! And . . .
you creatures . . .' he trailed off, then remembered
his purpose. 'Ah! How great is your father?
Don't answer that, boy. How great is the man
who sees the predicament his family is in, and
leaps into action to save the day? There, on the
brink of disaster and destitution sits the Otherhand

clan, and into the arena of doom strides the hero of the hour, the great one who will save the day, your Lord and saviour! Moi!'

He bowed low before us. Flinch sighed but was good enough to provide a weak round of applause. The children, though used to this sort of address from the man that other children would have called 'Dad', just stared blankly at him.

'Behold!' cried Valevine, a wild look in his eyes. 'Here it is! The machine that will save us all from wandering the streets asking kind ladies for spare bananas – my Mark One Gold Detecting Gadget.'

He bowed again and waved a hand at the contraption.

A penny dropped inside my dark and feathery brain-pan. There was some degree of logic in his antics. It is well-known, at least according to legend, that somewhere in the Castle there lies a hidden horde of fabulous treasure. Known as the Lost Treasure of Otherhand, this haul of loot is believed to have been tucked away hundreds of years ago, even pre-dating Otherhand possession of this ancient place.

It's rumoured to consist of a stack of gold, oodles of precious stones, and a prize diamond, called the Luck of Otherhand.

The trouble is, no one really knows if it exists, and if it does, where it is. The Otherhands themselves have no notion where it might be, and have mounted many unsuccessful expeditions to locate it. And even these failures do not deter the odd trespasser from straying across the Castle's boundaries of a dark night, spade in hand, for no one knows whether the treasure is in the castle itself, or somewhere in the grounds.

'Yes,' Valevine exclaimed. 'By lunchtime our crisis will be over! And we will all be worryingly wealthy. Well, I will be, but I'll see you all right.'

He winked.

'But how does it work? I hear you ask.'

No one had, but he was not to be deterred.

'As you can see, it is very simple. It is based on the concept of attraction. As you know, opposites attract. Just think of your mother and me. Opposites! So what we have done is placed a small sample of the thing that is *least like gold* inside what we call the "sensing pod" of the machine. Stop me if this gets too technical for you, by the way . . . The machine then will be drawn, like a magnet I say, to the presence of gold. Ha! Gold!'

Solstice considered what her father had said.

'What's that, Father? What's most unlike gold?'

Valevine seemed to hesitate for a moment.

'Hum. Well, we're not exactly sure, but we've got our suspicions. Oh, yes, indeed we have. We've got a shortlist, and we just need to work our way through it. We're starting with plums, sausages and bird mess. No offence, Edgar old boy.'

I glared at Valevine but he was already fiddling underneath the device. He turned to Flinch.

Flinch nodded, and reached out one long bony finger. He flicked the smallest and least important-looking switch, and all of a sudden the Gold Detecting Gadget burst into life, fizzing and sucking and popping and humming all at once.

'Away we go, man! Away we go!'

And they were gone, away and out of the

front door, a fortune just waiting to be found.

Seven

The music room
is a sadly neglected
corner of the castle
where beautiful and
ancient instruments
gather dust.
Sometimes though, a
gentle, ghostly tune
can be heard from the
music room, even
though no one's there.

The moment had come.

The situation had escalated.

And once again, the body count had started to climb in Castle Otherhand.

First, a footman was found in the cellar.

Next, a housemaid, duster in hand, was found rigid in the library.

Third, a boot boy, turned as white as his polish was black, sitting on the back kitchen steps.

It seemed that I had been wrong! The castle was infested with ghosts! Ghosts that had to be got rid of! Forthwith!

Solstice stood on the threshold of one of many doors that led into the South Wing. This one was on the third floor, and was not one that Valevine had boarded up. He'd got bored after about three doors, and had then just wagged a finger at us all, forbidding us to enter the South Wing from that time hence.

'Gulp,' said Solstice. 'I'm quite nervous, now I come to think of it. Will you be a brave bird?'

Since I was sitting on Solstice's shoulder, there was no need for me to speak too loudly.

'Kor,' I said gently. I knew it was bad

for Solstice, from the way she'd said 'gulp', and not 'gasp'. When she says gulp, it's serious. Really serious.

We peered into the gloom of the South Wing.

Beyond, a corridor led away into dusty darkness.

'Gasp,' Solstice added, reassuring me slightly. 'I think I might need my torch already.'

She was right. Even though we were setting out on a sunny late summer morning, the windows of the South Wing were shuttered, sealed and coated with dust and cobwebs.

Solstice rummaged in the satchel and pulled out the torch. She slid the switch and shone the light into the dark. It seemed a very feeble beam indeed, but she whispered into the musty air.

'Come on, then. Let's find the . . . You-Know-What.'

We crept along that first corridor, and maybe I imagined it, but I think the beam of light was a little wobbly in Solstice's hand.

About halfway down the corridor, I decided to suggest something to her.

'**Arruk**,' I said, which meant, actually, do you know, that after all I think I might rather *not* come on this expedition but could I still have one dried mouse for getting this far?

Solstice seemed not to hear me, and pressed on.

We explored.

We came to the end of the corridor, a nasty and cold place with odd people staring at us from paintings. They were presumably ancient

Otherhands, and though I remembered some of them, many I did not. Every one looked like a total fruit-loop, it must be said. At last, the corridor opened into a largish room.

It looked as though no one had been there for five generations, which was entirely possible. Three doors lay in the far wall, each of them shut.

Solstice flicked the torch about the room. There was not much there. A chandelier covered in spider webs, some more paintings of very odd things and even odder people. A single dining chair standing in a corner of the room made it look more empty than if it actually had been.

Looking at the three doors, Solstice hesitated.

'Maybe I should make some notes. If
we're going to do this properly.'

She gave me a weak smile, and pulled out
the notebook and the pen from her satchel. She
tried to hold the torch under her neck, while she
held the book in her left hand and wrote with

her right, but it was a hard job to get the light pointing at the page.

She struggled for a while, then the torch slipped. She managed to grab it before it hit the floor, but then the book dropped, and the pen too, which rolled away into the dark.

'Bother,' she said.

She set her shoulders back and I fluffed up my feathers.

We looked at the three doors.

Solstice stepped over to the nearest, and put her hand on the doorknob. No sooner had she touched it than the wood of the door disintegrated, leaving Solstice

standing holding a brass door
knob in mid-air. The wood
had simply been waiting to
collapse, having rotted
where it stood for a
hundred years or more.

'Gasp,' said Solstice.

Beyond lay a bedroom,
and it was a very spooky
place indeed. An
antique bed lay
made up in the
centre. The corner of the covers
was even turned down, as if someone might
enter the room and go to bed at any moment.

'Edgar,' Solstice whispered. 'Do you

think that's where the ghost sleeps?'

I wasn't sure. Suddenly I realised how little
we knew about what we were doing, but
Solstice wasn't to be stopped now that
she had started.

Solstice flicked
her torch to a painting
on the wall, and rubbing
away some cobwebs, read
from a small plaque
screwed into the frame.

'"Lord Arthur Berbitude Frontage
Otherhand, beheaded in a freak wallpaper
accident." Gasp! Poor man . . . Edgar, maybe he's
Cudweed's ghost! Beheaded.'

We moved on, from room to room, and

all the while, it grew darker and dustier. From time to time the floor creaked frighteningly underneath us, and though I could have flown to safety if need be, I didn't fancy doing it in the dark after Solstice had fallen down a hole many miles deep.

We pressed on, and we pressed on, and a creepy business it was.

In room after room I wished my imagination was not quite so good. Were those cobwebs tickling us, or ghostly fingers? Was that just the floor creaking, or the bones of some old skeleton? More than once I heard the sigh of a dreadful tortured spirit. Or was it, as Valevine would have us believe, only the wind?

But as time ticked by, we had to agree

that we had actually found nothing more ghostly than a family of spiders living in a sock drawer.

I felt a familiar rumble in my feathery belly, and began to wonder how long we'd been exploring for.

I think the same thing must have occurred to Solstice, because she chose that moment to break out the snacks. Sandwich for her, desiccated rodent for me.

We munched in silence, thoughtfully.

'Edgar,' Solstice said. 'I think I'd better turn the torch off, just while we eat. Is that okay?'

It wasn't in the least bit okay, but she did it anyway.

'Forgot spare batteries,' she said in a small voice, and then I heard her swallow nervously.

'Just think. In the dark, there could be any old You-Know-What right here and we'd never know.'

It crossed my mind to ask her how that remark was helpful in the circumstances, but I concentrated on chewing my mouse instead.

The torch flicked back on, and we realised that its beam was perhaps not as strong as it had been before, and even then it had been rather frail.

'Maybe,' Solstice said, 'maybe we've done enough You-Know-What hunting for one day. What do you think, Edgar?'

I cawed loudly, and the mournful echo from the heavy stone walls of the South Wing was enough to tell us she was right.

So we began to retrace our steps, and I think it was about then that we realised that we might not exactly have remembered which way we'd come. Not for the first time, I got the feeling the castle was in a tricky mood and had led us astray. Deliberately.

Solstice had the brilliant idea of following her footsteps, literally, as they were clear enough to see in the thick dust on the floorboards, even by torchlight.

And that's when the torch went out.

Eight

A page from the
castle account:
Outgoings: four
maids, two bootboys,
new glass for the
rotunda roof, dried
mice, monkey litter,
oil for Valevine's
machinery.
Incomings: none.

I do not want to speak much of the remainder of the time we spent in the South Wing. As you might have guessed, I'm proud of my role as the true guardian of Castle Otherhand. I like to think of myself as the brave and noble protector of everyone who calls Otherhand their home, everyone apart from Fellah, obviously. But in that dark and foul set of passages, I was absolutely terrified.

How we made it out, I shall never know. Our one saving grace was my raven sight, so sensitive that I can see in almost utter blackness. After the torch went out, my night vision kicked in, and I was able to see, just a smidge. I flitted ahead from room to room, calling to Solstice all the time, so she knew where I was. She followed on behind, calling back to me anxiously.

'Edgar? Are you still there? Edgar?'

'Kawk!' I would cry, and **'Ark!'**
so that she knew I wouldn't leave her.

And somehow, after many hours of random shuffling, we emerged blinking into the castle proper.

'Gasp!' said Solstice, after a minute or two. 'It's nearly supper time. I'll be in such trouble.'

We ran (she did, I flew. Ravens don't run unless there's a *very* rare combination of circumstances) along the corridors of the third floor, steaming towards the dining hall before the seven o'clock bells could announce that supper was served.

Solstice knew well that if her father found out where she'd been, there'd be a lot of stern talk and finger wagging.

It was a minute to seven as she put on a burst of speed and charged into the dining room, sliding on the polished wooden floor as she did. But she needn't have worried.

There was no one there.

It took us five minutes to find everyone, and there they all were, crowding round something in the kitchen.

Or rather, someone.

'Who is it?'

'One of the maids?'

'Which one?'

'Does it matter?'

'Only for the undertaker's forms.'

'Oh. Madeleine, I think.'

'Madeleine Mary-Jane?'

'No. Madeleine Trixi Helena Loretta Jo-Jo L'Amour.'

'Right. Gotcha.'

At this point, Cudweed heard me flapping on to a tabletop and turned to see Solstice arriving close behind.

'What's going on?' she asked.

'Haven't you heard?' Cudweed asked. 'It's one of the maids. Scared to death. Totally snuffed it. Frightened by the . . . by the You-Know-What . . .'

'Futhork!' I declared.

'Gasp!' said Solstice. 'All that time, we were wandering around the South Wing, and the naughty You-Know-What was scaring the life out of people right here!'

I felt a deep and dreadful foreboding in my belly, and it wasn't just because I'd only had one miserable mouse all day.

Dark times lay ahead at Castle Otherhand, dark times indeed.

Nine

One of Minty's
spells from her
witching days – a
cure for boredom:
A spoonful of
chicken cough
A whisker of
beaver breath
A pinch of bottom
A dash of moonlight
Three free-range eggs.

The castle was divided. Half were now utterly convinced in the existence of malign but ethereal beings within the walls. The other half denied it. I myself sat on the fence. By Spatchcock's shed. At the bottom of the garden. But I was really in two minds about the whole business.

On the one hand we had a spooked monkey, a nervous boy, a dead kitchen maid, plus the footman and other assorted victims. Looked at like that, it seemed a pretty clear-cut case of an evil supernatural inhabitation. But then, well, it wouldn't be the first time that a maid has been found laid out on the kitchen floor stone cold, all snuffed and gone.

Cook's rum punch has seen off quite a few of feeble constitution, to say nothing of her Marsh Toad Mash.

Furthermore, Cudweed is always nervous. The only time he's not nervous is when he's out and out terrified. And as for the monkey . . . well, if you haven't grasped by now that the monkey is a total loon, I haven't been doing my job properly.

So on the one hand, maybe we were all to be scared featherless in a matter of a few short days, but on the other, perhaps everyone was just getting carried away, as usual.

Sometimes the only way for a bird to clear his head is to have a jolly good flap. I tipped off the fencepost, and began to ascend into the heavens.

Dusk was falling, but I was in no particular

hurry, and besides, my rate of climb is not what

it once was. Now when I was a young chap I could

have made ten thousand feet inside six minutes,

but these days it takes a little longer.

After an hour or so then, I was well and truly aloft, and gazed down on the early evening scene in the valley. The sun had been beyond the Western Hills for a good while, yet it was a clear and cloudless night, and there was a purple glow that spread a deliciously eerie pall across my view.

I turned and wheeled, wheeled and turned, and gave the odd flap if I felt my wings going stiff. There was the castle nestled into the eastern wall of the valley, and with my extra-good bird vision, even from this height I could make out Valevine in his lab, making adjustments to the Gold Detecting Gadget. It transpired that Day Five of Gold Hunting had not gone so well. Rather like days One to Four, in fact. He and Flinch had been dragged round the grounds behind the demented shopping trolley, growing ever more convinced that they were closing in on the loot, until it had hurtled down the lower lawns and into the lake.

It had taken the rest of the day to drag it out again.

I could also see a flicker of candlelight beyond Solstice's small octagonal window.

She was up late, reading most probably, or writing some more impressively miserable poetry. There was no light at Cudweed's window. Poor chap, probably exhausted after all the frights of the last few days.

Right, I thought. Time for a spot of head-clearing.

It's a simple but effective way of getting your brain working.

First, you fly to ten thousand feet or so.

With me so far? Good.

Then, you tilt your beak down and your tail feathers up.

And then you stop flapping.

What happens is that really pretty quickly you find yourself in a full-on plummet, heading for the ground. Well, the exhilaration from those kinds of speeds is enough to get the old blood cells racing round your brain case, let me tell you.

It was a superb plummet, too, definitely doing the job, and then, as I plummeted, I suddenly noticed something odd. I saw lights in the castle, but what was odd was that they were in a part of the castle where no lights should have been. They were in the South Wing!

As I watched, I saw that the lights were most unusual; they were green and flickery and altogether most unearthly indeed.

I was captivated by the lights, and disaster nearly struck, for I'd forgotten that I was dropping like a stone. Suddenly I smelled lake and pulled up at the last second, fighting my way into a banking

turn that nearly pulled my wings off with the
G-force. It seems to have become a habit of mine,
getting a bit forgetful in old age, maybe.

Even in the dark I noticed I'd lost a
feather to the inky waters of the lake, and gave

rueful smile. I can't afford to lose too many tail feathers; it's all going a bit thin back there as it is, if you know what I mean.

Slightly glum, I flapped low across the water, heading back for the castle, brooding over the meaning of freaky lights in the South Wing at night.

I came to the wild conclusion that it could only mean the castle was being taken over by hordes of malicious spirits from beyond the grave, and as it turned out, I wasn't far off.

Ten

Cudweed is not
a great reader,
but he's determined
to finish
'Secrets of the Great
Taxidermists'
if it kills him.

'Eeeeeeeeeeeeeeeeeeee!'

This was the sound that greeted me as I swooped around the castle walls looking for a way in. I'd dallied a bit and it seemed I might be locked out. But as it happened the scream came from somewhere beyond the castle itself, and I hurtled about the walls trying to pinpoint its source.

'Eeeeeeeeeeeeeeeeeeeee-eeeee!'

The scream came again, and then stopped dead, but at least I had located from whence it came. Heedless of the fear coursing through my blood, I pointed the black spike on the front of my face towards the stable block and accelerated like a raven twenty years my junior.

I was too late!

Curse my aging wings and thinning feathers!

I was too late.

I arrived in the stables to find the horses a-whinnying and a-stomping, in total panic. Steam stormed from their nostrils and sparks flew from their shoes, and they looked like a vision of demonic mayhem.

Ah! And then I saw the cause for all this commotion. At the end of the stalls stood a stable boy. For a moment it crossed my mind to wonder why he was standing very still, open-mouthed and wide-eyed, and then I

realised he was the latest victim of the You-Know-What.

Scared to death where he

stood in his quaking little boots!

Thinking the Ghostie could only have left the scene of the crime moments before, I shot out of the far end of the stalls and took a quick circle around the stable block itself.

Nothing.

The spirit had vanished into thin air!

I took a couple more turns to make sure and then returned to the stable to find Flinch on the scene, along with Cook and a gaggle of gabbling staff. I was relieved to see that the infamous Nanny Lumber was missing from this gathering, still bed-ridden after the accident with a rogue trouser press. Hateful woman that she is, she would have only inflamed the situation even more.

As it was, there was quite enough pandemonium.

Everyone was standing round the still-warm stable boy, pointing and generally gasping in a way that Solstice would have approved of.

'Who is it?' someone whispered dramatically.

'New boy. Not sure.'

'He had a funny name,' someone said. 'Halibut or something.'

'Oliver?'

'That's it!'

'Look at his hair! Straight up!'

'Coo.'

At this point, Minty arrived in a swirl of elegant river-green silk, and sent everyone packing apart from Flinch and Cook.

'Flinch, my man,' she said. 'Would you do the honours? There's a tea chest in the store room that will fit this unfortunate mite until Box and Sons can come in the morning. Cook, will you speak to the agency again? It seems we are getting through staff rather alarmingly fast!'

The two faithful staff went about their business, and I decided to announce my presence to Lady Otherhand, because I sensed she was on the brink of brooding.

'**Ark!**' I said loudly, and flapped down to perch on a post at Minty's bejewelled right hand.

'You're quite right, Edgar. Quite right. Bless you. What a good boy you are! But you know,

Edgar, I fear for our very survival here, I really do.'

I noticed that Minty was still clutching needle, thread and a scrap or three of black velvet everywhere she went, which she then flourished at me.

'Ah, yes! You clever bird. You've guessed, haven't you? But you can keep a secret, can't you? I don't mind telling you that this little thing here is going to save us all from hideous poverty! Isn't that wonderful!'

She waved the mess of sewing at me and beamed.

Then her face fell.

'Of course, there is still the problem of the You-Know-What. But you're a clever bird. Let's do a deal. I'll save us from destitution, and you save us from the ghost. Yes?'

With that, she turned and went back into
the castle and I flapped after her before I got
locked out for the night.

Eleven

The castle has
its own cemetery,
tucked up on the
mountainside, a
short climb from the
vegetable garden.
Spatchcock the
gardener attributes
the success of his
prize cabbages to
the run-off from
the graves.

'What exactly,' said Solstice to her little brother Cudweed, the following morning over breakfast, 'did your ghost look like?'

'You mean the You-Know-What?' asked Cudweed, tickling Fellah's ear in an effort to get him to perk up a bit. He was still very much out-of-sorts.

Solstice sighed.

'Yes, very well. The You-Know-What.'

Cudweed swallowed hard, and looked wildly around him.

The children were having their breakfast in the nursery as usual. It's Minty's firm belief that it is instructive for Fizz and Buzz to see how their elder siblings behave at the breakfast table. The terrible toddlers, however, were attempting to flick egg yolk at me, which meant I had to move perch every few minutes, as their aim improved.

I hatched a few evil thoughts about leading them to the lake and waiting for a big pike to swim by, but most of my attention was taken by Cudweed's description of the ghost he and the monkey had seen.

'Well, it's been coming back to me,' Cudweed said, sounding slightly frenzied. 'And I think . . . I think . . . I think it was scary. No, I know it was scary.'

Solstice sighed again.

'Yes, but what did it look like?'

'Oh!' said Cudweed. 'Oh! I see what you mean. Well, for one thing, I could see right through it. Right through. And it was all white and floaty.'

'Hang on,' Solstice said, 'If you could see right through it, then how was it white?'

Cudweed blinked.

'I don't know. It just was. White and floaty. But you could see through it too. But it wasn't invisible or I wouldn't have seen it.'

The word is 'translucent', but I thought I'd let them prattle on anyway. At least the boy was finally being of some use, though it worried me that Solstice was asking all these questions.

Was she planning another outing of the Ghost Hunters to the South Wing? I hoped she wasn't.

'And did it float in the air, or did it walk along the floor?'

'I don't know,' said Cudweed, 'but it was a he, and he was very scary.'

'Why? Why was he scary?'

'Well, you see, he had no head. Or rather he did.'

Solstice was on the verge of screaming herself now, and I wouldn't have blamed her.

'Well, which was it? It can't have been both.'

'I mean,' Cudweed said, as if explaining something to a very dim and sleepy rabbit, 'that he had a head, but not on his shoulders. He was carrying it under an arm.'

'Gasp,' said Solstice seriously. 'That *is* scary.'

Cudweed nodded.

'So he was white and floaty, but maybe walking, and had his head under his arm. What was he wearing? Old-fashioned clothes?'

Cudweed nodded again, harder this time.

'Yes, old-fashioned clothes. He had a top hat on his head. Under his arm. If you see what I mean.'

'A white top hat?'

'Yes, he was all white. I told you that.'

Solstice fell silent.

The silence lasted for about five seconds and then there was an ear-splitting wail from somewhere below us.

We all froze, except Fizz and Buzz.

I turned towards the direction of the scream, straining for any further clue and then a large blob of egg yolk landed on my head.

'Naughty Buzz,' said Solstice.

Fizz chuckled. Vile infant.

We shot out of the nursery and along the corridor to the grand staircase. I led the way, nobly ignoring the egg dripping down my lovely glossy black feathers. Solstice scampered close behind me. Bringing up the rear by some way came Cudweed, caught between fear of being left alone and fear of whatever lay ahead. Personally I would have thought that Fizz and Buzz were enough to scare off any poltergeist or apparition, and that Cudweed would have been perfectly safe had he stayed behind.

We reached the gallery at the stairs and peered down into the Small Hall.

The wail came again, indistinct at first, and then louder as a maid ran across the hall as if her apron strings were biting her bum. There was a great clatter and bang as something came after her, something on wheels, with wires and tubes and smoke and steam all fighting for attention. Really though, no maid who's worked in the castle for more than a month should be unaware of Valevine's inventions, and their unreliable and frequently dangerous nature.

'Oh,' said Solstice. She turned to beckon Cudweed over for a look. 'False alarm! It's Father's Gold Detecting Gadget again. It seems to be detecting kitchen maids today.'

Another wail rose from
the hall, followed by an almighty
crash as the machine ran headlong into a suit of
armour that stood by the front doors.

Faintly we heard Valevine's voice drift up
to us.

'Flinch! Cross watercress off the list. It
appears to be the opposite of shrieking young
female. Not gold, no. Reset the device and let's
try the next item on the list. Hmm? What? Yes,
that's what it says. What? What's strange about
that? Sardines? Perfectly feasible.'

We left them to it, and stalked back to
the nursery.

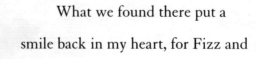

What we found there put a
smile back in my heart, for Fizz and

Buzz had
not wasted
their time
while unobserved
by anyone larger
and more
sensible.

Fellah was dancing
and dodging on the table, but in vain, for he was
covered from head to toe in egg yolk.

The twins giggled.

'Oh, Fellah!' cried Cudweed.

Solstice tried not to laugh, but I couldn't

help a small comment.

'**Arrak!**' I said.

'That's right,' said Cudweed. 'And you know

what this means, don't you, Fellah? Bathtime.'

At that, the ape lost his sandwiches

entirely and began to freak like a frog at a disco.

'You know the rules, Fellah,' said

Cudweed. 'Nobody likes a sticky monkey.'

Twelve

Solstice has been
trying to read up on
witchcraft in her
mother's old spell
books. The trouble
is the writing is so
bad it's never clear
whether a spell is to
make the victim fall
in love, or turn them
into a badger.

By the end of the week, the Scared-to-Death toll had mounted worryingly. Now you will have realised that this sort of thing is not entirely unknown at Castle Otherhand, but the frequency of visits by Box and Sons was remarked upon by Cook, who had to provide cupcakes and mugs of teas every time they called.

I had had a little flash earlier in the week. You know what I mean. One of those moments when everything becomes clear. And in that little flash I saw that once again, I, Edgar the brave and awfully smart, would have to save the day.

Valevine was occupied with his oversized gadget, Minty with some unsuccessful sewing. Only I could provide the answers required, and the first step, I knew, was to understand the enemy.

Until and unless we knew exactly what kind of ghostie and how many we were dealing with, there could be no solution, and so I set myself the unenviable mission of undertaking a twenty-four-hour vigil around the length and breadth of the castle.

I may have had the tiniest of naps now and again, but otherwise I was alert and aware at all times.

As news of the latest haunting came in, I sped to the scene like a feathery guided missile, ready for action and whatnot. But each time, I was too late. The translucent terror had vanished.

Things went on like this, day after day, and I knew that I must get ahead of the game. It was no good reacting to the victim's screams, for the victim was already a victim by that point. What I needed to do was to happen upon the ghost, or ghosts, *before* they did their dastardly deed.

In order to do this, I would need two things: a lot of luck, and silent and invisible cunning.

Now the second of these, I could manage, because without wanting to embarrass myself, I have to tell you that being silent and black is something we ravens are very good at indeed, when the occasion calls for it. I knew I could glide noiselessly and unseen around the gloomiest corners of the castle, and not even the ghostliest You-Know-What would have a clue I was there. As for the luck, well, I made a small raven prayer to the castle itself to lend a hand. Pitch in, do something useful, be a sport, for old times' sake.

So, I began my stealth mission; like a shadow I moved unseen and unknown.

Meanwhile, the hauntings continued, and I'm afraid to say, left a trail of victims behind. Three maids found clutching each other in a terror-death-grip. A pastry chef turned as white as his flour. And a gardener's boy discovered in a pile of leaves, only his boots protruding.

I missed all the attacks, and I had begun to despair, when finally, I had my lucky break. Maybe at last the castle had decided to do the decent thing and steer the ghost in my direction, or vice versa.

Whichever way you look at it, it happened like this.

Late one evening, I sat above a doorway, on an ornamentally carved arch, on the fifth floor, Northern Quarter. It was a peaceful and moonless night.

All was dusk and shadow, and I passed myself off as an avine addition to the architrave.

In other words, I pretended to be part of the fancy carving above the door, an idea I got from a poem which Solstice once read to me, educated girl that she is.

I had decided that rather than flap about the battlements like a psychiatrically disturbed bat, it would serve my purpose just as well to play a waiting game. It also allowed me to have a short snooze or two. Two birds, one stone. Sometimes I even impress myself.

And thus it was, as I drifted in and out of fondly reminiscent dreams of courting the late Mrs Edgar, that something reached up and touched me as I perched above the doorway. Now I don't mean that it actually touched me, but something tickled my sense of smell as I dozed, and I knew that someone, or something, had just passed underneath me.

Carefully, ever so carefully, I opened one of my coal-black eyes, then the other, and it was all I could do not to fall off the door right then and there. I held my frantic little raven breath, and tried not to gasp.

Immediately below me in the room stood a ghost. Now, the first thing I knew was that it was a different one from the one that Cudweed had seen, for this ghost still wore his head in the traditional way, shoulder-bound.

His back was towards me, but still I could make out some details. It was some kind of monk-based ghost, with a long habit sweeping the floor, and a big hood pulled up over his head.

Round his waist the habit was tied with a string of beads, and he carried a Bible in one hand. And, just like Cudweed's ghost, he was all white from head to toe, and gave off an eerie glowing light.

He'd walked, or rather floated, right under me, and was passing across the room, when suddenly he stopped.

I heard my heart thumping against my wishbone, and then to my horror, the You-Know-What turned.

I froze, staring straight ahead, but I was rumbled. Slowly, so slowly, the ghost raised his head to look at me.

His was truly the most repellent and frightening face I have ever laid eye upon; his

mouth gaped toothlessly at me, his eyes were
green fire and, worst of all, hair sprouted from
each of his ears like a vegetable garden.

His toothless mouth formed into a circle.

'Boo!' he said, and that was enough for me.

I shot past his head, far too close for comfort, close enough to get a good whiff of ghostly niff, but was free.

I didn't stop flying until I bumped into the back of someone, Solstice as it turned out, on her way to bed.

'Ow!' she said, turning round. 'Oh, Edgar. It's you. You made me jump.'

I opened my beak to say sorry, but found I had lost my voice.

'Why, Edgar, what's wrong? Why are all your feathers fluffed up? You look like a furry football. Edgar, is it what I think it is? Have you seen the ghost, too?'

'Futhork!' I said, and fell in a faint on the floorboards, a badly bedraggled bird.

Thirteen

Minty's To Do list:
Get ovens cleaned
Kitchen floors washed
Flue unblocked
Call Box and Sons
Dispose of mess
Employ new
kitchen maids
(three might be best
at current rate of loss).

'**W**ell,' Valevine announced. 'We have learned one or two things.'

He had called an extraordinary family meeting, which is a rare thing indeed, and showed just how low things had become.

The family stood in an untidy circle in the Small Hall. Fizz and Buzz were the prime culprits for the lack of perfect circularity, and Cudweed and Fellah a close second. Flinch and Cook had also been called as senior staff, though Nanny Lumber was still abed, I'm more than glad to say. We left Grandma S where she was, in bed at the top of the castle. No one could quite be bothered to go to the effort of hauling her downstairs.

'We have learned that our dear home is under attack from unknown rambunctious

apparitions with no sense of decency whatsoever.
And we must do something, but what?'

Valevine paused and I think he was actually
hoping someone would tell him, but no one did.

He coughed.

'And Flinch and I have learned one or
two things,' he went on, and patted the handle of
the Gold Detecting Gadget. 'For example, we now
know that the opposite of cheese is woodworm,
and the opposite of marble is curtains. I don't think
we saw that one coming, did we, Flinch? Eh?'

No one seemed to know what to say to
this, except Cudweed, who asked in a small
voice, 'Father, what's the opposite of monkey?'

Valevine ignored him.

'So we've learned one or two things, and

although it gives me a great deal of pain, I have decided for the imminent survival of the human inhabitants of the castle, to put my gold detection on hold!'

At that moment there was a rattle at the door and a bundle of letters plopped through on to the mat. Valevine sighed loudly.

'Post!' called Cudweed, and went off in the way that small boys do, expecting mail order goodies even though they haven't ordered any.

He returned looking slightly glum.

'Why is there never anything for me?' he asked the world in general.

'Because you never write to anyone or

send off for anything,' said Solstice, who happily took the latest copy of her subscription from Cudweed. It was a magazine called *The Dark Pen: Ghoulish Poetry by Correspondence Course*.

'There are some more of those letters from Lichtenstein,' Cudweed announced, and Minty snatched the whole bundle from him. She flicked through them, snipping with her scissors and dropping all the snippets one by one into the fire basket. Suddenly she stopped and slid a long and razor sharp fingernail under the flap of an envelope.

Her faced darkened.

'It's from the agency,' she said. 'They say that if we keep losing staff at this rate then they'll have to double the fee! Outrageous! Who do they think they are? Blackmailers!

Mountebanks! Swine!'

She went on in this manner for a while, and then fell silent, flicking through the rest of the letters.

Lord Otherhand meanwhile had become a touch grumpy, having been about to deliver one of his famous proclamations and being denied his minute of glory.

'If I may continue!' he snapped, then composed himself. 'As I say, I am prepared, though it wounds me deeply, to turn my attentions from the pressing issue of gold detection, to the even more pressing matter of spirit removal. And therefore, I have decided to employ this marvellous machine of which I am justifiably proud, and turn it to a new purpose.'

'What's that, Father?' asked Solstice, almost interested.

'Aha! Indeed. What is it? Simply this. We will turn the Gold Detecting Gadget into a *Ghost* Detecting Gadget, simply by changing the sample in the sensing pod from that of the opposite of gold, to the opposite of ghosts! Genius, no? In a matter of minutes we will have found the ghost, and evicted it from our realm!'

Minty was reading. Feverishly, if such a thing is possible. Cudweed was half-listening and half-tickling Fellah. Flinch was staring into space and Cook was trying to remember what sort of flour to use in the recipe for Mustard Muffins.

It was left to Solstice and me therefore to question the wisdom of Valevine's plan.

'But, Father,' she said. 'What *is* the opposite of ghost?'

Valevine had perhaps been expecting this question, for he seemed to know the answer.

'Well,' he said. 'What are ghosts? Describe them, if you will, daughter of mine.'

Solstice thought briefly, then said, 'They're invisible, light and floaty, and very scary.'

'Exactly! And what is the opposite of that?

What do you know that is totally visible, heavy, and not at all scary?'

Solstice thought for a minute and a half, at the end of which she shrugged in defeat.

'I can't think of anything.'

Valevine had hatched an evil grin and had stalked around behind Cudweed. He clapped a hand on his shoulder, and winked at Solstice.

'Are you sure you can't think of anything?' he said. 'Totally visible, heavy and not in the least bit frightening?'

'Father!'

'Valevine, you will not put our son in that ridiculous gadget of yours,' Minty said, looking up from her letter. 'As it happens, I have solved the problem myself. Talking of letters, I received a circular in the post a few days ago, from a wonderful man called Spookini, the Great Ghost Hunter. By our very good luck it seems he's in our neighbourhood, and is hunting ghosts. I wrote to him and have engaged his services. This is a letter from Spookini in my hand, and he promises to arrive this very morning to aid us in our predicament.'

I must admit that sometimes the old girl has a flash of rational, sensible and totally practical thinking, and it seemed she had now pulled off this precise feat.

At that very moment, there was a ring of the doorbell.

'Ah!' cried Minty, ignoring the scowls on her husband's face. 'That sounds like him right now! Our troubles are over!'

Fourteen

Despite having a
pet monkey, Cudweed
has expressed a
desire for a hamster
too. Minty has
refused on the
grounds that she's
rather worried about
what he might do
with it.

I 'm told, though I find it hard to believe, that some people find ravens a little bit scary as birds go, a touch threatening perhaps, and that some people see us as birds of ill omen and all-round badness.

Now let me take this opportunity to set things straight. Ravens are the loveliest birds you could wish to meet, every one a true gentleman or a delightful lady. A more charming bunch is impossible to imagine.

And yet look at the names we've been given: a *murder* of crows, for example, or an *unkindness* of ravens. Is that fair? I assure you it's not, and if you've ever spoken to a raven, or even a crow in general for five minutes, I'm sure you'll have come away thinking what an altogether

decent fellow he was.

I mention this in passing to say that generally I always greet a newcomer to Castle Otherhand with an open mind and a warm heart, and yet, when Captain Spookini, the Great Ghost Hunter stepped over our threshold, I took an instant dislike to him. And I wasn't the only one.

For one thing, he had entirely too many teeth in his head. Now you might think this is a bit much coming from someone who is entirely without dental arrangements, but if you'd seen him I think you would have agreed.

His whole face was governed by the teeth thing. His eyes were pretty normal, though maybe a touch too close together. His nose was thin and sharp but I can hardly complain about that, can I?

But his mouth was remarkable for the size, irregularity, and outright quantity of teeth that seemed to want to fight for pole position every time he opened it.

He was wearing what I took to be typical Ghost Hunters' clothes: riding boots and jodhpurs, starched white collar, tweed waistcoat, hounds'-tooth overcoat, and some sort of military cap. On his breast was pinned a medal, which presumably had something to do with the 'Captain' business. In his hand he carried a large leather briefcase.

No sooner had Flinch flung the door back on its hinges than the Great Ghost Hunter strolled into the Small Hall as bold as you please.

'Lord and Lady Otherhand, I presume?' he chirruped.

Valevine scowled and began to fiddle with his gadget, but Minty stepped forward. In a single motion Spookini swept Minty's outstretched hand up into his own and planted a toothy kiss on the back of it.

'Enchanted,' he intoned. Minty arched a single perfectly shaped eyebrow.

Spookini turned his attention elsewhere, to Solstice and Cudweed.

'Right, kids?'

Well, that was enough to set Solstice scowling as hard as Valevine. Cudweed just blinked a couple of times, and then said, 'This is Fellah. He's my monkey.'

This almost threw Spookini for a moment, then he grinned.

'Really neat, kid,' he said, and the use of such slang was enough to make Valevine snap his fingers at Flinch and begin to haul the soon-to-be Ghost Detecting Gadget back upstairs.

Now Spookini plucked his cap from his head and bowed low.

'Captain Horace Spookini, the Greatest Ghost Hunter known to man or spirit. At your service. I shall require little during my stay. Some peace and quiet, three meals a day, a modest room

with bath. Preferably with a view of the valley. And in a day or so, your ghostly problems will all be over.'

'No need,' muttered Valevine loudly from the stairs. 'All sorted. Got the machine, you see. Thank you. Goodbye.'

Spookini spun on his heel and stalked over to Valevine and Flinch.

'And what is this thing?' he asked rudely.

'This, sir,' said Valevine, his goat really got now, 'is a miracle of human engineering. A versatile piece of kit, it will imminently be reborn to the world as a Ghost Detecting Gadget. Which is why I say to you, no need. Thanks all the same. Sorry to have bothered you. Door's over there.'

Spookini seemed totally unmoved by this,

and took a couple of steps back to his large leather bag.

'That thing is not a Ghost Detecting Gadget,' he announced. 'It is some kind of mechanical disaster on wheels. What you need when hunting ghosts is purpose-made gear. You need the right gadget. And it just so happens I have the very thing.'

He rummaged briefly in the bag and pulled out a natty, sleek, handheld device – a long shiny tube, with no more than two switches on it. It looked rather like Solstice's torch, if somewhat more sophisticated.

'Observe!' Spookini declared, and flicked a switch. Immediately the machine began to emit a small beeping sound, slow but regular. Spookini swung the sleek gadget this way and that, and as he did so, the beeping came and went. Finally, with a dramatic gesture, he flicked the switch off again.

Now he had everyone's attention, even Valevine's.

'Interesting,' Spookini said, as if there was no one else there. 'Very interesting.'

Minty's interest was sparked, I could see. I think she was perhaps reminded of some of the witchy things she used to get up to as a young woman.

'What is it, Captain?' she asked.

'You have ghosts in your castle.'

'Oh, bravo,' retorted Valevine sarcastically.

'Shh,' said Minty. 'Do go on, Captain.'

Spookini grinned with many, many teeth.

'You can call me Horace,' he smarmed.

'But yes, indeed. You have at least three ghosts here. A Level Three poltergeist and possibly a couple of basic apparitions. And a very smelly bird. Maybe something worse. This could be more serious than I thought.'

'Ooo,' said Minty. 'Most interesting!'

'Oh, for goodness' sake,' said Valevine, and with that he stomped off upstairs with Flinch, their machine slung between them.

Unnoticed, Solstice had already disappeared, and I flew off to look for her. I wondered if her feelings were the same as mine, and I determined to find out. Smelly bird indeed! How dare he!

Thoughts whizzed round my feathery brain.

Whatever had become of Castle Otherhand?

Ghosts! And gadgets!

Fifteen

Minty got her nickname at witch college. While other girls were messing around with henbane and hemlock, Euphemia seemes to like nothing better than a nice cup of fresh mint tea.

Captain Horace Spookini did not begin his investigations that day, saying he was tired from his long journey, but fortunately the ghosts took a day off too, and we lost no more staff of any description.

'I don't like it,' said Solstice, that afternoon.

She and Cudweed were sitting at the table on the High Terrace again, munching on scones, muffins and teacakes. I sat a short distance away, keeping one eye on the table, in case it tried anything funny with my beak again.

'You mean you don't like *him*,' said Cudweed, which was an unusually smart remark for the boy.

'All right then,' said Solstice. 'I don't like him. "Kids!" Hah!'

'Is that all?' asked Cudweed.

There's the teeth question, I thought, but Solstice was ploughing right on now.

'Isn't that enough?' she demanded.

Cudweed nodded.

'I suppose so.'

'And anyway, Father's going to find the ghosts with his device!'

Touched as I was by Solstice's sudden devotion to her father, I was also slightly worried that she might be exhibiting a hint of the lunacy which so plagues Otherhand kind.

'If he can find the opposite of ghost,' said Cudweed, then added in a hurt voice, 'Apart from me, that is.'

'Yes,' said Solstice, 'That's right. Maybe . . . I have an idea . . . maybe we could . . . help him?'

'What? With his invention?' said Cudweed. He looked worried. 'I'm not sure that's a good idea, Solstice.'

For once I had to agree with him. Fellah was still slinking around like a frightened mouse, and while I wouldn't want you to think that my attitude towards the monkey was softening in anyway, it did show just how peculiar things had become in the castle.

'What we need to do,' said Solstice, 'is think really, really hard. And then maybe we can find the opposite of ghost, tell Father, get his gadget to work, and we can get rid of Captain Spookini.'

'But why don't we just let Captain Spookini get rid of Captain Spookini,' said Cudweed. 'Mother's paid him something already anyway. We may as well let him do his job, get rid of the ghosts, and then life can go back to normal.'

Normal? I thought. Define *normal*.

'But,' said Solstice, 'he's not doing his job, is he? He's making himself at home in the guest wing.'

'He's tired,' protested Cudweed. 'After his long journey. And he has to get ready for tomorrow, he said.'

'Is that why Cook's baked five times this afternoon already? To keep him well fed?'

'Well,' said Cudweed, 'it's not as if we haven't benefited from the bakery ourselves.'

He grinned greedily at the table, and so did I. But I wasn't going to risk a foray just yet. I was keeping an eye out for cracks.

Solstice smiled and helped herself to

another scone, which she began to smear with blueberry jam.

'True,' she said, between mouthfuls. 'But I have to say that the buns are not up to Cook's usual standard.'

'That's because she's run out of the normal flour. She told me when I was in the kitchen that she would have to use wholemeal and we weren't to complain.'

'Do you know what though, Cudweed?' Solstice said, chewing thoughtfully. 'How do we even know that Captain Spookini is what he says he is?'

'What do you mean?' asked Cudweed, eyes wide with alarm at the very idea.

'Well. How do we know he's the Greatest

Ghost Hunter known to man or You-Know-What?'

'He has certificates,' Cudweed announced. 'I've seen them. He showed me.'

'He showed you? You've seen them?'

'Yes,' said Cudweed. 'I've seen them. I went along to his room to see if he liked monkeys and he showed me all these certificates he's won for being really, really good at finding ghosts.'

'And getting rid of them?'

'*And* getting rid of them. Of course, getting rid of them. That's the whole point isn't it? And I think you should just let him get on with the job tomorrow morning when he says he's going to start and let him find the ghosts and get rid of them and then maybe my poor little monkey will be happy again.'

Solstice opened her mouth, then shut it again. It was quite possibly the longest sentence Cudweed had ever uttered, and it showed how worried he was about the smelly primate known as Fellah.

'Very well,' said Solstice. 'We'll let him do his job. And I'll be keeping a close eye on him.'

That's my girl, I thought, an Otherhand to the core.

Suspicious and nosy.

Sixteen

The family rarely
makes excursions
to other places, but
when they do, they
travel in style, in a
large coach pulled
by four large, black
and somewhat bad-
tempered horses.

Some people get ravens. Others don't. That is a sad fact, but fortunately the ones who get ravens, *really* get ravens. Would you allow me to occupy a few minutes of your time on Earth by telling you just a couple of the many thousands of ideas that people have had about ravens? You would?

Oh, good!

Well, for instance, it was the warriors of the Ancient Far North whose god Odin had two ravens as guides and protectors. They were called Huginn and Muninn, and they flew out from the castle every morning and returned every evening to perch on Odin's shoulders and give him the news. Their names were understood to mean 'thought' and 'memory', and they were Odin's eyes and ears.

It's for that reason that I like to think I might descend from those fabulous birds of so long ago, because I am the eyes and ears of Otherhand Castle, just as Huginn and Muninn were of Odin's Hlidskjalf.

But on the particular morning when Captain Spookini embarked upon his Ghost Hunting, I was reminded of another of the many ideas about ravens. And it was this. It has been said that the reason the raven has become such a familiar character in all the mythologies of the world is because he serves as a messenger between the world of the living and the world of the dead. That we drift along the borderlands separating these two places, and can look either way, into the light, or into the darkness.

So say the most learned thinkers upon the high renown of the raven. And there was me thinking it was because we were rather cute.

As Captain Spookini paraded himself in the Great Hall, readying to do battle, I was reminded of my role as a communicator between life and death. And as much as I disliked Spookini, I wasn't going to let him work unobserved.

So. We were going to go a-ghosting.

Brrr. It made my feathers itch just to think of it, but there was no backing out! Solstice had decided that we would follow Spookini every step of the way, she and I, and that's what we prepared to do. Although, having said that, Solstice was late. She was the last down for breakfast and had not been seen since by brother, mother, or favourite raven.

I watched Spookini make his final preparations, and the few assembled servants made little 'ooh' and 'ahh' noises as he flourished this implement, or brandished that gadget.

He sported the same clothes that he'd arrived in, with an additional item: a pair of goggles such as one might wear when driving a vintage motor car. For the moment they balanced on his cap, but he had spent a good quarter of an hour polishing each lens, muttering 'must get these infra-ultra-radio-polarising-ghost-goggles clean', and occasionally 'dirty ghosts!'

He seemed ready finally to depart into the South Wing, when

all in a fluster, Solstice arrived on the scene.

'I'm here,' she said, rather unnecessarily, 'and ready for action!'

She did indeed seem ready for anything, from invasion by a foreign power, to an Antarctic penguin hunt.

She was dressed in black combat gear from head to toe. Gone were her stilettos, to be replaced by big black boots with reinforced steel toe-caps. Her hair was tied up in a bun and shoved under a large black furry hat. Gone was the Ghost Hunting satchel, and in its place, she had a stylish black rucksack on her back. I believe the word is 'nifty'.

'I've got spare batteries this time, Edgar,' she said, winking at me, 'and a couple of extra mice.'

'Wo-ho! Woah! Wait up there! Hey.'

Captain Spookini choked as if swallowing a hedgehog.

'What's your game, kid?'

I winced, but Solstice put on her brightest smile.

'I'm coming with you. To find the You-Know-Whats. And ask them to leave.'

'That's sweet, kid,' said Spookini, 'but there's just one problem. I work on my own, see? Tod Sloan. Alone. Solo. Geddit?'

'But I want to help,' Solstice protested. Adding, 'Edgar's been looking forward to it.'

'No can do,' said Spookini. 'Not up for

debate. Please note Clause Fifteen, Point Four of the contract your mother signed.'

He fished in his own bag of gear, and waved a fat sheaf of papers at Solstice in a most insulting way.

'I don't care,' said Solstice, 'I'm coming with you. I've got sensible shoes on and everything. And, Mother, you know how much I hate sensible shoes.'

'Now, dear, listen…' Minty began.

'I'm off,' said Spookini, but he didn't mean for the South Wing.

He packed up his stuff and started for the door.

'No! Wait! Mister, I mean, Captain Spookini! Horace, please!'

Minty fluttered after him.

'Do please go about your business. I apologise for the rudeness of my daughter. She won't be coming with you. I've got a lot she can help me with today anyway, and you obviously need a little peace and quiet in which to work. Wouldn't do to frighten the ghosts away, would it?'

Wouldn't it? I thought. Isn't that exactly what we want to do?

Captain Spookini stood by the door, one hand on the doorknob.

He sighed like a troubled actor, then dropped his chin and pointed all his teeth at Minty.

'Lady Otherhand, I thank you. Have no fear! I shall not let you down!'

And with that he was gone, this time down the long hall towards the South Wing, and I for one hoped we'd never see him again.

Sadly, this was not to be the case.

Seventeen

Solstice reads a
lot, though her
choice of reading is
fairly narrow. Her
favourite book, a
typical example, is
'Death Wish of the
Creepy Ones'.

'**W**ell!' declared Solstice. 'How rude!'

I flew over to her and began to pull her hair out from under her big furry cap.

'Yes, I suppose you're right, Edgar,' she said. 'It does look better down, doesn't it? But you know what . . . ?'

Her voice dropped to a whisper and she beckoned Cudweed over. Fellah scampered along behind him, still a faint shadow of the abominable ape he usually is.

'Just because,' murmured Solstice, 'he says we can't go with him, doesn't mean we can't go wandering round the South Wing ourselves, even if we're not supposed to. And if it so happens that we go the same way he has, well…'

She winked at her brother, who

blinked repeatedly.

'What? You mean, follow him?'

'Shh! Mother's coming.'

'What's that?' barked Minty, coming over from instructing some domestics in the day's business. 'Nothing? Well, now. Follow me. We have work to do, just in case you have any foolish ideas. I need your help with snipping and stitching and so on, Solstice.'

'Mother!' Solstice protested. 'Sewing!'

'And go and change out of those ridiculous clothes first,' Minty added. 'I ask you! A daughter of mine in trousers!'

She shuddered.

'Oh! Really!' cried Solstice.

'What about me, Mother?' asked Cudweed.

'Yes, well,' said Minty. 'Yes, well, you can . . . watch.'

'Watch? Sewing? Watch sewing?'

Cudweed's eyes opened so wide with horror at the prospect that they nearly left his skull.

Nevertheless, that is exactly what happened.

Minty, Solstice and Cudweed spent the day on the High Terrace in the sunshine.

'Nights will be drawing in soon, children! Take the air while we can!'

Spread out on the table this time was not a feast of Cook's baked delights, but dozens of pieces of black velvet, strewn this way and that. Minty's sewing basket sat at one end, most of its contents spilled across the top of the other mess. Solstice sat gloomily by her mother who ignored the sulking and sang a little song to herself.

Cudweed sat at the far end of the table, with Fellah curled up on his lap. I hardly dare bring myself to say it aloud but I began to grow, well, somewhat concerned for the monkey. Now don't get me wrong, I'm *not* going soft. But I was missing having my old adversary to spar with, you know. Not the same without your arch nemesis on the case, is it? That's all.

Fizz and Buzz were doing their usual double act, climbing out of their playpen when they thought no one was looking (I was) and getting into various varieties of mischief.

Buzz was crawling along the battlements, quite unseen by his mother, with only me pecking him from one side to prevent him dropping a few hundred feet to the lawns below.

'Now you see, my dear daughter,' Minty was explaining, 'that I do have this simply wonderful idea but I can't make it work because I'm afraid to say my fingers are too big. But you have lovely dainty fingers, so you can sew up these fiddly bits that just won't behave.'

'This is the pattern, is it?' Solstice asked vaguely, trying to get interested, but failing, I think.

'That's it. Off you go.'

Cudweed was picking at some bundles of white fluffy stuff near him on the table.

'What's this?' he said, his boredom so bad that even white fluffy stuff had become mildly diverting.

'Ah ha!' said Minty. 'Just you wait and see if your clever sister can do the first bit. Then you'll see.'

For a moment I was almost interested myself, then I realised Fizz had joined Buzz on the battlements, and I had double pecking duties.

'Mother,' said Cudweed. 'Are the twins supposed to be up there?'

'Hmm? Oh, no. I suppose not,' she said, somewhat distracted, and plucked and returned the devilish duo to their playpen, where they began to mewl and pucker.

She came back to the table.

'Ah! Yes, that's it. Yes.'

'But what is it?' Solstice moaned.

'Well, you need to turn it inside out, like so. Then a little of this white fluffy stuff, here. Up we go! And then. I can do this last bit. A couple of stitches here. And there. And . . . voilà! What does that look like to you?'

Solstice gasped.

'Gasp!' she said.

Cudweed blinked.

'It's … it's…'

'Yes?'

'Gasp! It's a little Edgar!'

Well, that got my attention. It was true, the batty old girl had actually designed a small fluffy stuffed toy replica of, well, me. From its

tiny wonky beak to proud little tail feathers, it was undeniably Edgar-shaped. I felt a little bit funny inside. Most odd thing indeed.

Cudweed clapped.

'He's funny!' he cried, then looking at me added hurriedly, 'In a good way, I mean.'

'He's so cute!' said Solstice. 'Oh, Mother, you are clever! Only…'

'Yes, child?'

'Well, you've bought yards of this material and bags of the fluffy stuff, and he's tiny. Why do we need so much stuff?'

She was right. The little Edgar was no larger than Solstice's hand, at the very most.

'Well, you don't think we're only going to make one, do you?' Minty said. 'We're going

to make dozens, hundreds. Lots and lots.'

'But why?'

'To sell them, of course! To make money!
To save the castle and all who sail in her!'

'Gasp! Mother, you're actually quite clever.'

'Yes, dear, now get sewing, because I have
calculated that we need a thousand by the end of
the week. Let me just see if I can use this one to
keep your little siblings quiet for five minutes.'

Off Minty went to dangle the miniature
version of myself at the twins, and I have to say the
tiny fluffy me did a jolly good job. And very soon
Solstice had made a second one, and Cudweed had
made himself useful doing the stuffing. Minty sewed
up the final stitch as before and then there were two
miniature Edgars to keep both Fizz and Buzz happy.

Well, after that, scissors snipped and needles dipped and within an hour or so there was a table full of tiny fluffy black ravens, each and every one with a wonky beak.

'Keep up, Cudweed' cried Solstice, shoving another raven skin towards him. But Cudweed had stopped.

'What's wrong?' Minty enquired.

'Well, it's just that,' he said. 'It's just that you said we were going to sell these things and make money and save the castle.'

'Yes?'

'Well, who are we going to sell them to?'

There was silence, and as the penny dropped in Minty's head, her face fell too.

'I hadn't thought that far,' she said shakily.

Without further ado, she stumbled miserably away from the High Terrace.

Solstice sighed.

'Sometimes, Cudweed, I swear we are a totally stupid family.'

Speak for yourself, I thought, and decided to see if the pile of tiny Edgars made a comfortable nest. It did.

Solstice looked glumly at me wallowing among the soft, black fluffiness.

'You may as well, Edgar,' she said. 'You may as well.'

'Hey,' said Cudweed suddenly. 'I wonder how Spookini's getting on.'

That put a sly look on Solstice's face.

'Good point!' she said. 'I'd almost forgotten about the You-Know-Whats.'

'The ghosts, you mean?' said Cudweed, and Solstice looked at him strangely.

'Yes. Ghosts. Now a thought occurs to me, oh brother of mine. Namely, if we're not now needed by Mother, and if Mother is furthermore no longer watching us, then there would be nothing to stop us from seeing what progress the great Ghost Hunter is making. Would there?'

'Apart from the fact that I'm terrified?'

'Apart from that, yes.'

'Well, I suppose you're right,' Cudweed agreed, swallowing hard. 'But only till tea time. And the first sign of any You-Know-What, and I'm running like crazy. Okay?'

'Okay,' nodded Solstice, grinning like a tipsy tiger. 'Now, we just need to find a maid to look after these two and, Cudweed, I think perhaps it might be best if Fellah went to his cage for a while, yes?'

'Yes,' nodded Cudweed sadly. 'I think you're right.'

So!

We were back in action! And I made ready by flapping my wings a bit and cawing happily.

As we left the High Terrace, I peered in at the twins, who had fallen awfully quiet. I soon saw why. Both were fast asleep in their little orange-and-black striped romper suits, each of them sucking on a toy raven nose.

That, I thought, is rather endearing, but

is only going to lead to greater wonkiness of beak.

Eighteen

Minty's
Shopping List:
Little black dress
Streaks for hair
Flea repellent
(monkey and
raven varieties)
Blood stain remover

'But how will we find him?' Cudweed puffed, as he struggled to keep up with his sister, who is much fleeter of foot.

'We need to traverse the castle as fast as we can!' Solstice cried. 'Cover as much ground as possible. And be a little bit lucky!'

I made a silent address to the castle.

Did you hear that? We need you on our side, so try and be helpful for once.

'I know!' called Cudweed. 'We could use our roller skates! And Edgar can fly, and we'll whiz round the corridors.'

'Great idea!' Solstice agreed, and they ran to their bedrooms. Sadly for Cudweed's brilliant plan, neither could find their roller skates, so we set off on foot instead.

It was starting to get towards late afternoon, and the sun was setting over the Western Hills. We scurried along towards the South Wing, unnoticed by any human eye, at least.

Soon we found ourselves, torch in hand, setting foot and talon where only the brave dare venture. Even Cudweed managed to go fifteen minutes without his teeth chattering, but pretty soon we realised the impossibility of our task. The castle is simply enormous, and we were just a bird and two roller-skate-less children.

We gave up.

I cursed the very stones for their lack of help, and we slunk silently back into the castle proper.

As we came around a corner near the

guest wing, however, we were in for a surprise,
for who should we find there but Captain Spookini!

His back was turned towards us, and for
a good minute he didn't realise we were there.
I perched myself on the helmet of a suit of armour,
and we watched fascinated as he went about
his business.

He lifted the carpet that ran down the
corridor, peered at the floorboards for a while,
then let the carpet fall back in place. Idly he lifted
a few pictures from the walls, then set them back
on their hooks. He poked his
nose behind a drape or
two, and then knocked
very quietly on some of the
wooden panelling.

It was at this point that he turned round.

He jumped slightly to see a raven, a skinny girl and a chunky boy all staring at him.

'Ow, kids!' he said eventually. 'All right? How long have you been standing there?'

'What are you doing?' Solstice asked.

'Ghost Hunting, of course,' Spookini replied, too smoothly for my liking. 'What do you think I'm doing?'

'Ghost Hunting?'

'Smart kid,' said Spookini, nodding and flashing teeth around as if they were easy to come by.

'Behind paintings?' asked Solstice.

Spookini didn't seem to like that.

'Who's the ghost expert here? You, or me? Eh? Kids?'

And with that he turned and stomped off.

'See you at dinner,' he called over his shoulder.

We did indeed see the great Captain Spookini at dinner, though it was a strained business. Spookini rambled on to Minty about the close shaves with spirits that he'd had during the day, while Valevine muttered that the only spirit Spookini had been near came in a bottle and said 'twelve years old' on the side.

That sent Spookini off on a jibe about the overly large nature and doubtful functionality of Valevine's Ghost Detecting Gadget, which really frosted the atmosphere nicely. Minty did nothing to break the ice that was rapidly forming, because she was still sulking about not having anyone to sell toy Edgars to. Apparently she had made a vow never to do anything practical ever again, and just stick to totally useless and impractical fads.

Solstice and Cudweed glared at their soup, and glared at the wholemeal rolls they were forced to eat with it, and the whole thing didn't end nearly soon enough.

At bedtime, I sat with Solstice as she did some pondering.

She sat in bed under black silk sheets decorated with embroidered shrunken heads, reading from a big book all about ghosts and hauntings and monsters and such flim-flam.

'Do you know, Edgar, there's definitely something wrong about that man.'

I didn't need her to tell me who she was talking about. Finally the humans were coming round to my way of thinking.

'Yes,' she mused. 'Definitely something

amiss. Why would you look for ghosts behind paintings? Or under carpets? I can't find anything in my book about supernatural rugs . . .'

'Aaa-arrk,' I said, agreeing whole-heartedly. Something was certainly wrong, but I couldn't quite put my beak on it.

'And my book is quite new, and it mentions all the great Ghost Hunters: Alfonso the Bold, who found and dispatched a thousand You-Know-Whats, Henry Hirsute, whose whiskers twitched when a poltergeist was near, Lady Samantha Sloop, Ghost Hunter to royalty. It doesn't mention Captain Spookini anywhere.'

'Ur-rurr,' I pointed out.

'Hmm? Yes, well, I started to think. You know, Edgar, don't you find it odd that Spookini just happened to be in our neighbourhood, just when we have a problem with ghosts? Isn't that odd? A little bit too convenient, if you see what I mean?'

'Futhork!' I cried.

I did see exactly what she meant.

And if that is indeed the case, then heaven help the man when I am through with him.

Bring (I thought, using the latest and most modern expression) it on!

Nineteen

The fame of the long Lost Treasure of the Otherhands has spread over the years. The infamous robber Sneaky Pete once travelled six hundred miles to have a crack at it, but even he went away empty handed.

Wicked and sly looks were exchanged betwixt Cudweed and Solstice over breakfast, but only when grown-ups weren't looking. I however, being a generally all-seeing sort of bird, saw everything.

A plan was being hatched, and I have to say that I very much approved.

Straight after breakfast, Spookini announced that he was hot on the trail of the ghosts and would have more information to report at dinner time, and could he please have some extra sandwiches to keep him going as no one fully understood what tiring work it is hunting apparitions.

With that, he disappeared along a second floor corridor towards the South Wing.

Solstice had a plan, and she'd spelled out our roles to Cudweed and I. It was my duty to be the eyes and ears of the operation. The Huginn and Muninn of Otherhand Castle, as it were.

I was a deadly, silent sleuthing stealth operative, a shadow among shadows, a whisper on the wind, a phantom, a ghost indeed!

I had been sitting utterly invisible on the bust of Lord Deffreeque overlooking the Small Hall, and as Spookini set off, I slipped from my perch and glided down the corridor, to where Solstice and Cudweed were waiting. Both were dressed in black. For Solstice this was not unusual, I concede, though it was a new look for Cudweed, who generally mucked about trying such wild colours as grey and brown.

I have to say black suited him.
Made him look less . . . well, just less.

'Ready?' asked Solstice.

'**Urk!**'

Cudweed nodded.

'Edgar, you know your job?'

'**Urk!**'

'And I will follow close behind
with my instant camera. If we catch
him up to anything, we'll soon prove it to
everyone.'

'**Urk!**' I agreed, wondering if we
were going to get on with it.

'And, Cudweed, you know your job?'

'Hang around towards the back and try
not to knock into anything?'

'Excellent! Then let's go.'

We turned and were almost thwarted at once. Behind us, Lord Valevine and Flinch had trundled less-than-silently on to the same landing that we were occupying.

We froze, conscious that with every moment Spookini was getting further away, and we might never find him again.

Valevine flicked the Ghost Detecting Gadget into neutral and regarded us suspiciously.

'And where are you three going?' he enquired. 'Not got any plans about following Spookini into the South Wing, have we?'

He looked at us very seriously indeed.

'Oh, no!' said Solstice. 'Absolutely not. Have we, Cudweed?'

'No! South Wing? You know how I hate You-Know-Whats, Father.'

Valevine nodded.

'Good. But what's the camera for?'

Solstice changed the subject.

'How is your machine getting on, Father?' she asked cleverly.

'Excellent! Superb! Not at all bad!'

'Have you found the opposite of ghost yet?' asked Solstice. Cudweed himself was nervously looking at the sensing pod and wondering which bit of him his father might try and stuff in there if he got the chance.

'Yes,' declared Valevine. 'That is. Not quite. We thought we were on to it yesterday, but . . . however, we do now know that the opposite of custard is fossils, and the opposite of air is glue.'

'But ghosts . . . ?'

Valevine shook his head sadly.

'Maybe,' said Solstice. 'Maybe it's just something you haven't tried yet. I'm sure you'll find it.'

'Yes, my dear,' nodded Valevine glumly. 'But if that damned Spookini finds the ghosts first, I'll never hear the end of it from your mother. Cudweed, where's that chimpanzee of yours? I've half an idea to try monkey paw in the sensing pod.'

'No!' cried Cudweed.

'Well, I just thought . . . ah well, no matter. If you change your mind come and tell me, there's a good boy.'

Flinch and Valevine trundled away down

the hall, discussing what object to place in the sensing pod next, and as soon as they were gone, we sprang back into action.

'You know,' Valevine called as he went, 'you should have called that monkey of yours Coat Hanger.'

'Why's that, Father?' asked Cudweed foolishly.

'Because they both spend all their time just hanging around.'

A 'heh-heh-heh' came echoing down the corridor, which is odd because Grandma S was nowhere in sight, though she does like a bad joke very much indeed.

'Very funny,' muttered Cudweed, but only after Lord Otherhand was out of earshot.

There was not a moment to lose! If Spookini's trail had gone cold, our mission would have to be postponed for another day, in which who knows how many weak-hearted serving staff might be frightened into an early grave!

Twenty

Solstice's most
recent poem is
a short one:
'If I were dead,
I wouldn't be
sad, and I
wouldn't be
glad, because I
wouldn't be.'

What we found that morning did indeed chill the blood, but then, strangely enough, made it boil. Let me explain, for I fear my feathery little raven brain is getting all tangled up.

I set off ahead of Solstice and Cudweed, and was soon rewarded by the sight of Captain Spookini on the threshold of the South Wing. I veered round and back out of sight, landing at Solstice's feet.

I pointed my beak around the corner and Solstice nodded.

'Excellent work, Edgar,' she whispered. 'Let's just give him a minute, then we'll pursue him.'

I could tell Solstice was feeling herself again when she used a word like 'pursue'. Full of excitement and drama!

'Solstice?' whispered Cudweed. 'How am I doing?'

Solstice smiled.

'Excellently, also. You haven't bumped into anyone or anything yet and we've been going nearly five minutes.'

We counted to sixty, and then I peeked around the corner. He was gone!

We trotted after him, as silently as we could, and into the South Wing we went.

It grew dark, but we didn't dare risk the torch, so I led the way through the gloom, and the children followed.

It didn't take very long at all before we spotted him.

It was about then that I began to smell

something. It was not a bad smell by any means, but it was quite distinctive, though subtle. It was something I had smelled very recently and I began to wrack my brain for any clue as to where and when.

My thoughts were deep and mysterious then, as Spookini moved on. We trailed him to the very edge of the next corner, and once again I poked my beak around and had a quick look.

Now this was the point at which my blood chilled.

For what I saw was not Spookini.

What I saw was You-Know-Whats.

Two of them. One was the Mad Monk I'd seen a few days before. The other was equally horrific, a lady ghost, white dress, white hair, bloody hands, very, very scary.

My small raven heart began to thump against my ribs and I ducked back.

If I had been Solstice, I would have said 'gasp!' but being without the power of human speech (it's to do with lips and larynxes) I could only let out a small and mournful 'urk!'

Solstice understood, and Cudweed, and then all three of us plucked up our nerve and poked our heads around the corner.

There they were, the blood-chilling ghosts! And then, then came the blood-boiling bit.

For Spookini emerged from some far corner and stood, looking at the ghosts.

Even stranger, he began to talk to them. Then he began to argue with them, though we really couldn't hear what they were saying.

The two ghosts seemed very upset.

Spookini meanwhile
was delving in his briefcase,
and pulled out a small
white bag.

Yes! That was it. The
smell came back to me.

Flour. Spookini had just
given them a bag of white flour.

Most odd. Then he
pulled out some sandwiches

and handed them round to the ghosts as if it was a buffet reception.

The ghosts stopped arguing and sat down, and it was at that point that the hems of their clothes were pulled up, and we were able to see their feet for the first time, which was most odd, for each of the ghosts appeared to be wearing roller skates.

'Solstice?' whispered Cudweed. 'Are those *our* roller skates?'

'Shh!' warned Solstice, but I had to agree with Cudweed. I was now very much of the opinion that the ghosts might not actually be ghosts at all.

'Right!' said Solstice. 'When I say "run",
then run. Or in your case, Edgar, you might be
better off flying. Now, shut your eyes.'

Thanks for the tip, I
thought, but then there was
no time for thinking any
more as Solstice poked her
camera at the three
figures, and pressed
the button.

There was
a blinding flash.

'Run!'
cried Solstice, and
we did. Having
closed our eyes, we

weren't blinded by the flash as the three interlopers were, and we made good our escape.

But we could hear a great clattering and banging as our pursuers chased after us.

We put on a burst of speed, and anyway, this is our castle. There's the odd secret passage that isn't so secret.

We lost them, and before too long found ourselves panting and brow-mopping on Solstice's bed, inspecting the photograph.

'So!' declared Solstice. 'Impostors!'

Twenty-one

The top floor
and rooftops of the
south-western corner
of the castle are
dominated by huge
glass houses, in
which grows a
jungle of strange
and fearsome plants
and trees. It's a
dangerous place, but
a good one to visit
on a chilly day.

The photograph was blurry and very small, but it was clear enough, and showed Spookini chatting to the You-Know-Whats.

'But what are they up to?' asked Cudweed, always last on the uptake.

'Isn't it obvious?' Solstice said. 'The ghosts aren't real. They're friends of Spookini's. They've been hiding in the South Wing, scaring half our servants to death, just so that we'd be in need of a Ghost Hunter!

'And then, how convenient that Captain Spookini happens to be in the area and announce himself to Mother!'

'But why?'

'Why, dear brother, it's obvious, because they, like many other people, are after the fabulous and possibly mythical Lost Treasure of Otherhand Castle. Don't you see? That was why Spookini was more interested in hunting behind paintings for hidden compartments than in looking for ghosts!'

'Ahh,' said Cudweed expressively. 'We could do with the treasure ourselves.'

'Indeed,' said Solstice. 'But we have to get rid of these impostors first. Huh! What cunning creeps. Roller skates to glide around the floors to make it look as if they were floating. And the flour! They've been stealing all the white flour from Cook all this time.'

'You mean,' said Cudweed, trembling with rage, '*they* made us eat … wholemeal?'

Solstice nodded and Cudweed said a very bad word.

'What,' he asked then, 'are we going to do?'

'We're going to do the right thing for once,' said Solstice. 'We're going to tell our parents! With this photograph as proof, they'll have to believe us.'

Now Solstice is a bright girl, and I am quite fond of her, but I must admit that sometimes she does display dizzying lapses of judgement, and this was one of those moments.

For while it is a general rule among human kind that the best thing any child can do in a moment of difficulty is to tell their parents, Solstice had forgotten one thing; namely that her parents are not general human kind. They are demented, insane, idiotic lunatics with less grasp on reality than a sea slug.

And thus it was that when Solstice waved the photograph under Valevine's nose, he merely said:

'Quiet girl! This is a pivotal moment. Mustard or rotten eggs?'

And when she proffered said photograph to her mother, Minty simply stated:

'Can't you see I don't have time for this? If we don't get Cook some white flour soon, she's threatening to resign, and we'll never eat again!'

So by the time Solstice returned to sit dejectedly on Cudweed's bed, she was also fed up, angry and totally determined. She threw the photograph on to the floor.

'We have to sort this out ourselves, Cudweed. The grown-ups are too stupid.'

'Yes. But what can we do?'

He gazed mournfully at Fellah, who for the first time in his life actually seemed glad to be inside his cage.

It was at that

moment that I

noticed something.

I began to

peck madly at the

photograph as it lay on the floor.

'Quiet, Edgar,' said Solstice. 'We're trying

to think.'

Yes, I thought, and I'm trying to save our

skins. I pecked some more, and some more, until

I pecked enough so that they both understood

there was something about the photograph I

wanted them to see.

Solstice picked it up.

'What is it, Edgar? Have you spotted

some . . . ? Oh my goodness. Gasp, even! You *have* spotted something!'

She turned to Cudweed.

'Cudweed. I know brains are not your strong point, but how many ghosts did we see talking to Spookini when I took this photograph?'

'Two,' said Cudweed. 'And I resent that.'

'Never mind. Take a look at what Edgar's seen!'

He looked.

'Urk!' he cried, sounding a lot like me. 'It's a guh . . . a guh . . . a guh!'

Yes, urk indeed, for there in the background, hidden a bit behind Spookini so he was harder to see, was another ghost.

'Be brave, Cudweed! Is that the one you

saw?' Solstice asked her brother gently.

He nodded frantically.

'One that you can

actually see through, not just one

covered in flour? One that carries his head under

his arm?'

Cudweed nodded so hard I thought he might

be in danger of getting ants in his picnic again, but with remarkable restraint, he held it together.

'Gasp,' said Solstice. 'Then that, my friends, is a real You-Know-What.'

And with that, Cudweed did indeed faint, and I felt my feathers stiffen with fear, but Solstice stood up, looking noble.

'And I have a plan.'

Oh my goodness, no, I thought, but it

was too late for that. She had made up her mind.

What Solstice did next took some guts, I can tell you. I can tell you because I was the only witness to the scene that ensued, as we made our way once again towards the old South Wing.

Twenty-two

In the castle
grounds, to the
north, lies the
Mad Maze, composed
of seven miles of
towering box hedges,
many a foolish soul
has ventured in.
And never been
seen again.

When we finally emerged again, there was a huge uproar coming from the Great Hall.

Solstice and I appeared in the doorway.

'Ah!' cried Spookini, who appeared to be the centre of attention yet again. 'There she is! Your most rude and unfortunate daughter. It is slander and lies I tell you and I will sue you for every penny you have!'

Cudweed hopped up and down, waving the photograph at anyone who would listen.

'He's an impostor! Look! He's friends with the ghosts, only they're not really real ghosts at all. They're his friends.'

At last Valevine listened and scratched his head, and looked at the photograph, while Minty stood in a state of confusion, wondering if she should indeed throw Spookini out of the door with his tail between his legs.

Various serving staff who had heard the noise began to grasp what was going on, and were making all sorts of wild accusations at Spookini too.

'You will never get rid of your ghosts, not without me,' he cried wildly. 'You ungrateful bunch!'

'I thought we didn't have any ghosts,' said Valevine, fiddling with his gadget still. 'Or do we?'

Cudweed sighed and pointed at Spookini again.

'The ghosts are his friends!'

'Anyway, my dear boy, I think I've finally cracked it. The opposite of ghost. You see, you would be the opposite of ghost, but you know what your mother says about that. And you won't let me touch your monkey, but then I thought, well, as I said, what does your monkey do but hang around all the time. Like a coat hanger. So the opposite of ghost, is coat hanger. Quite simple. when you think about it.'

With that he shoved a fancy wooden coat hanger into the sensing pod of his machine and flicked it into drive. All at once the machine leaped into life.

Sadly, no one saw this triumph, because the row was reaching monumental proportions.

'You will all die in your beds!' Spookini sneered between molars and incisors. 'And you will deserve it. Scared to death by ghosts.'

At that precise moment, the Mad Monk and the White Lady flew into the hall, passing right by Solstice and myself.

There was the whiff of processed flour.

Quick as a flash, Solstice tripped the Monk and I plucked the hem of the White

Lady's
dress,
exposing
roller skates
as they
both went flying.

What they shouted next was most peculiar.

'Ghosts!' they cried. 'Ghosts!'

They dragged themselves over to Spookini,
and began to claw at his jodhpurs. Quite painful
I should imagine.

'Ghosts!' they wailed. 'Ghosts!'

'What's all this?' demanded Valevine.

'Poppycock? Tomfoolery?' added Minty,
in a most terrifying tone.

Spookini kicked his friends.

'There are no ghosts, you fools. You are the ghosts!'

But they would not stop, and then Solstice shouted quite loudly and clearly.

'Are you quite sure about that, Captain Spookini?'

Everyone looked at her, and then we stood aside as a tall white figure floated down the steps into the Hall. He was quite see-through, and wore a top hat on his head.

Spookini looked a little worried, but then recovered himself.

'You can't scare me with that,' he stated. 'That's just your butler covered in flour.'

'Is it?' said Solstice. 'Well, for one thing, Flinch is over there.'

She pointed, and Flinch bowed solemnly.

'And for another thing, Flinch is not see-through. And thirdly, Flinch is unable to do this . . .'

She nodded at the apparition, who opened his mouth in a big grin, then lifted his arms and picked his head off his shoulders. He floated towards Spookini, head held out before him, chomping his teeth fearsomely.

When he was only a few inches away,

the ghost of Lord Arthur Berbitude Frontage

Otherhand put his lips together, and said:

'Boo!'

We did not see Spookini, or his accomplices, for

dust. Or for flour for that matter, as they shot out

of the castle as if it were falling down around

their ears.

Everyone stared open-mouthed as the ghost put his head back on, and floated quietly back towards the South Wing.

As he passed Solstice, she curtsied very neatly.

'Thanks, Arthur,' she said, and the ancient Lord Otherhand winked.

'My pleasure,' he intoned in a very good ghosty way.

'Well, bless my soul,' said Valevine, who was being dragged along behind his machine, which was actually heading straight for his spooky ancestor.

'The damn thing actually works. Something I built *actually* works.'

Minty gave him a big kiss.

'I knew there was something wrong about that Spookini man,' she claimed lamely, but Valevine was too happy to care.

Fellah poked his head down from the second floor landing and began to chatter like, well, a monkey, and everyone except me was glad of his return to full fitness.

I looked at Solstice in wonder. Even I, the brave and noble raven, had quaked at the idea of returning to that bedroom we'd found in the South Wing, summoning its ghostly owner, and asking him for help.

But Solstice is quite the girl.

I hopped on to her shoulder.

'Well, Edgar,' she said, planting a light kiss on the tip of my beak, 'we might still be as poor as poor, but we'll always have each other.'

'**Urk!**' I cried, my little heart swelling with pride. '**Urk!**'

'And by the way, you have the straightest beak of any raven I know.'

Postscript

A few days after Spookini and his gang had fled the castle, Solstice and Cudweed were having tea, when suddenly Solstice realised something.

'Cudweed,' she said. 'You know, maybe you're not as much of a scaredy-puss as you think you are. All those servants got scared to death by fake ghosts. And you saw a real one, and lived! Maybe you're actually rather brave.'

Cudweed quite liked that thought, and puffed up a little with pride, as did his monkey, who, I'm very sad to say, had returned to his usual self. Annoying, loud, stupid, rude, and very, very smelly indeed.

**Following Ghosts and Gadgets, Edgar
reveals all in**

Lunatics and Luck
Magic and Mayhem
Vampires and Volts
Diamonds and Doom